I KNOW YOU'RE LYING

BY DAPHNE BENEDIS-GRAB

SCHOLASTIC INC.

All rights reserved. Published by Scholastic Inc., *Publishers since 1920.* SCHOLASTIC and associated logos are trademarks and/or registered trademarks of Scholastic Inc.

The publisher does not have any control over and does not assume any responsibility for author or third-party websites or their content.

This book is a work of fiction. Names, characters, places, and incidents are either the product of the author's imagination or are used fictitiously, and any resemblance to actual persons, living or dead, business establishments, events, or locales is entirely coincidental.

ISBN 978-1-338-79398-7

10 9 8 7 6 5 4 3 2 1   22 23 24 25 26
Printed in the U.S.A.   40
First printing, September 2022

Book design by Maeve Norton

FOR NGHIA

CHAPTER 1

NORA

"The following four students must report to the main office immediately: Nora Montgomery, Jack Tran, Henry Davis, and Maddie Fox."

Nora nearly dropped the packet of papers she was holding when she heard her name. That would not have been good. Thanks to a struggle opening her locker, she was running late to drop it off. And if the contents of the packet spilled and anyone saw—

"Uh-oh, Nora, what did you do?" a voice asked.

Nora shrieked with surprise and spun around. Tanisha and Grace were walking into the newspaper office and laughed at her reaction. As her heart slowed, Nora joined them—her reaction *had* been extreme. Usually before the first bell, the classroom used as a newspaper office was empty. That was why Nora was here—though today she wouldn't be able to accomplish her goal, now that she had company.

"Looks like you're in big trouble, getting called to

the office before school even starts," Grace said in a singsong voice, grinning.

"Like our star reporter would get in trouble for anything," Tanisha scoffed, walking over to Ms. Holt's desk to put an article in the paper's in-box. Although the *Snow Valley Secondary School Sentinel* was online, Ms. Holt preferred to edit articles on paper.

Nora tried not to appear too pleased by Tanisha's remark. She liked to project an aura of serious, cool calm at all times to fit her role as star reporter. Nora, who had been called "cute little thing" for far too long in life, much preferred labels like "star reporter." She subtly stuffed the papers back in her old-fashioned leather satchel. (Nora felt a reporter would carry a satchel, not a backpack. Plus backpacks made her look even shorter than she actually was.)

"She's probably getting an award," Tanisha said as Nora headed for the door.

"Nora, yes. Maddie and Jack, sure. But Henry?" Grace said, eyes narrowing slightly. "Nora, why are you and Henry both being called to the office?"

Nora shrugged, calm and cool, though she *was* slightly unsettled by that. And by the fact that she was being called to the office at all. "Principal Montenegro probably just needs to speak with us about separate things but called us down in a group," she said.

Luckily Grace, who was a good writer, did not have the instincts for a story that Nora had been born with. There was definitely more to the story here—and Nora was part of it. Not something she was feeling good about as she hurried out of the newspaper office and down the hall.

People were starting to trickle into the building now that the front doors had opened to students (Nora had slipped in early, as she always did on Wednesdays), and there were about four more minutes before the first warning bell would ring.

The walls of Snow Valley Secondary were covered in posters for next week's Starlight Gala. Nora had to take a detour past the science lab because the hallway leading to the auditorium was blocked off. That was where the displays of student art, schoolwork, and—most importantly—newspaper stories were posted for the Gala. There would be time for attendees to admire the work before sitting down in the auditorium for performances by the band, sports teams, and the crowning finale by the dance squad.

Nora's article on the upcoming town council

election, as well as her investigative series Behind the Scenes: Snow Valley Secondary's Cafeteria Unglazed, were both featured. Like most of Nora's stories, they had not exactly gotten much readership. But Ms. Holt had praised them highly, and hopefully the families who came to the Gala would appreciate her hard-hitting, extremely well-researched news reports.

As Nora turned the corner, she was nearly plowed down by a group of boys from her class.

"Sorry, Nora," one of them said as he grabbed her arm to keep her from falling. "I didn't see you there." She looked up at him—he was a full head taller than Nora. It was a boy named Rudy who she knew was on the basketball team.

His fellow jock friends laughed and Nora gave them a sour glare. She wasn't *that* short. And they were definitely over-tall, like most of Nora's classmates.

"Watch it, she'll write an exposé on you," Miles said.

"Yeah, Rudy, she'll *expose* you!" a voice shouted from down the hall. Henry Davis.

Nora rolled her eyes as Henry came loping over. He could always be counted on to say something stupid to make everyone laugh. She ignored them, straightened her satchel, and started toward the office again.

"Nora, hey, why are we being called in?" Henry asked, jostling her as he tried to join her. He seemed totally unaware of both the fact that he'd just pushed her and that his comment had annoyed her. Henry's other trait was being oblivious to the obvious. He had a small scratch on one cheek, pink against his white skin, and Nora would bet money he had no idea how he'd gotten it.

"I don't know why you're being called in," she said shortly.

Henry ran a hand through his messy, too-long brown hair and then tugged on it for good measure. "I don't think I did anything bad today," he said, though he sounded unsure.

Nora sped up, hoping he'd get the hint and leave her alone, but Henry just matched his gait to hers as they headed to the office. He was like a big, sloppy, and very unwelcome puppy.

Ms. Atkins looked up from her desk as they came through the door. Then something weird happened: She didn't smile at Nora.

Every adult in the school, from the teachers to the janitors to the administrators, always smiled at Nora. Always. Nora got amazing grades, raised her hand in

5

class, volunteered at every event, and was excellent at conversing with grown-ups (she was actually a lot better at speaking to adults than to her fellow seventh graders). So they were, without fail, happy to see her.

Except for right now. A cold, slithery snake began curling up in Nora's belly.

"Principal Montenegro is waiting for you in room 122," Ms. Atkins said, in a tone that could only be described as frosty. "Don't dawdle."

"Why room 122? What's even in room 122?" Henry babbled as he followed Nora, who nearly ran the short distance to room 122. It was a previously unused space that had been set up for small meetings, with a table encircled by office chairs and not much else.

Principal Montenegro stood at the front of the room, arms folded across her chest. She nodded at them as they entered but *did not smile at Nora.* The snake in Nora's belly was now nipping at her insides. She had to hold on to the table to avoid fainting. Something bad was happening. And Nora reported on bad things—she didn't take part in them.

"Please sit down," Principal Montenegro said, her voice ice.

Nora shakily sank into the closest seat. It was on

wheels and nearly slid out from under her, but she managed to land without injury.

"What's going on?" Henry asked as he pulled out a chair and rolled backward, almost crashing into Jack, who had just walked in. "Sorry," he said as Jack jumped back.

Principal Montenegro ignored Henry and glanced at the clock on the far wall. Across the table, Jack, who had taken his cue and sat, gave Nora a "what's going on" look. Jack drew for the paper, so they sometimes chatted in the newspaper office. She liked that he looked to her for answers now, and hated that she didn't have any. She shook her head, just as confused as he was.

Finally Maddie, a girl from the school dance team and the only person in seventh grade who had better math scores than Nora, stepped inside.

Principal Montenegro nodded. "Close the door, Maddie, and we'll get started."

Maddie looked slightly panicked as she shut the door and hurried to sit down, and who could blame her? Nora had never seen their smiley, warm principal act so remote. So angry. Even last year at the assembly when a student took over the PowerPoint presentation in an exposé that had gotten the last principal fired (Nora felt it had been a well-researched story but did not belong in a middle school assembly), Principal Montenegro had remained even-keeled. But not now.

The snake was attacking Nora's belly now, and she pressed a hand against it.

"As one of you is well aware, a student's locker was broken into this morning and an item was stolen," Principal Montenegro began, looking carefully at each one of them. Henry shrank down in his seat when the principal's eyes rested on him, but Nora just stared because this was not what she had expected. "The victim took it upon herself to report the incident to her mother, who happens to be president of the PTA. The mother is now threatening legal action, so this incident has become top priority."

Nora looked toward the door in panic.

"Are we under arrest?" Henry asked, leaning forward, his eyes big.

Principal Montenegro shook her head. "She is giving us the morning to correct the situation before reaching out to her attorney," she said in an iron tone.

"That's a relief," Henry said, sitting back.

Principal Montenegro glared at him. "It shouldn't

be. This set of events is a clear violation of school rules," Ms. Montenegro continued. "So whichever one of you opened Sasha Saturday's locker without permission and stole her backpack, I suggest you confess now." She leaned down, palms pressed against the table so that she was at their level. "The faster you tell the truth, the better this will go."

Nora's brain, which usually moved so quickly it sometimes gave her headaches, had stalled. Why was *she* here? Did Ms. Montenegro want her to write something for the paper?

"Um, I didn't do it," Maddie said. "I don't know if Sasha said I did or—"

"Did I ask who did *not* steal the backpack?" Principal Montenegro asked sharply.

Maddie blinked a few times. "Ah, no, but I'm confused why I'm here."

Although Nora prided herself on nerves of steel when investigating a story, getting in trouble with the principal was on a whole other level. She was impressed Maddie wasn't backing down. And really, why *was* Maddie here? Or Nora or Jack? They would never do something like this, and Ms. Montenegro knew it. It had to be Henry.

Except, why would Henry do such a thing? Sure, he

was a class clown who annoyed people, but he wasn't the kind of person to commit a crime. Was he?

"Last night when our head custodian, Mr. Smith, left the building, nothing was amiss," Ms. Montenegro stated. "But this morning when Sasha entered the building *with permission*"—she paused to give them a sour stare—"at seven twenty, she discovered her locker had been opened and her bag taken. She immediately informed her mother, who called us."

Nora found this odd. She would have told Principal Montenegro, not called Mom. But then, Sasha and Nora were about as different as two people could be.

"As you know, after the events of last year, our school installed a video camera at every entrance that goes on automatically when the door is unlocked," Principal Montenegro said. "The front entrance is opened at seven a.m. sharp, for faculty and staff only. The other entrances open at seven forty-five. So when we received the call from Ms. Saturday and surveyed this morning's footage from the only accessible door— the front entrance—we saw that four students came into the building before hours without permission: the four of you."

Nora gulped. She had come into school early,

"without permission" as Principal Montenegro said. But not to break into anyone's locker! Especially not the locker of Sasha Saturday, who was super popular and, when provoked, super mean.

"So if it was you, 'fess up now," Principal Montenegro said, straightening her shoulders and staring down at each of them.

A toxic silence fogged the room, threatening to choke Nora.

"All right," Principal Montenegro said. "If you won't reveal yourself to me, I will give you the opportunity to reveal yourself to your peers. All four of you are here on in-school suspension"—Nora gasped—"which will only go on one person's record: the person who committed the crime. Maybe the pressure from the three other people in the room is what you need to confess. I'll be back before the end of first period."

With that she strode out, leaving the four of them staring in shock at one another, the closed door trapping them inside room 122 together.

CHAPTER 2

JACK

"I didn't do it," Henry said, spinning his chair around in circles. "But I don't mind if whoever did takes a while to confess—I have math first period and we have a quiz."

Jack sighed. Unlike Henry, he took being locked up for an in-school suspension seriously. Plus he would be missing art, and art wasn't just a class. It wasn't even just something Jack did. It was who he was.

It also happened to be the root of his problem: He'd never have been at school early if it weren't for art and the mess it had created in his life.

"Anyone can say they didn't do it," Maddie said to Henry dismissively. "It doesn't mean anything."

Henry grinned. "So it didn't mean anything when you said it to Principal Montenegro?"

Jack didn't know Maddie well, though of course he'd seen her perform. The Snow Valley Secondary dance team only had eight middle schoolers and eight high schoolers, and was so good they won regional competitions. Their smaller, squad-team performance was the grand finale at the Starlight Gala, and this year it was being livestreamed by some YouTuber who was apparently a very big deal. All of which meant Maddie was basically Snow Valley royalty.

But in this moment she was glaring at Henry. "No, it means something when you say it to an authority figure, but not now, when it's just us. And you're the obvious suspect—it's not like Nora or Jack did it."

Henry grinned wider. "But you might have! You didn't rule yourself out."

Why was Henry so annoying all the time? "Just confess if you did it," Jack said shortly.

Henry shrugged, as if he didn't care one way or the other. "Like I already said, I didn't do it. But my guess is it's you—everyone knows you and Sasha don't like each other."

Jack's throat tightened, his breath sour, as the two girls turned to stare at him. The bell ending home-room rang and a moment later they could hear voices in the hall outside. Jack wished, rather fervently, that he was with them and not trapped in here.

"That's true," Maddie said slowly but not accus-ingly. "I've seen you guys arguing."

Nora sat quietly, but Jack saw the way her head was cocked slightly to one side, the intensity of her gaze as she took in the scene, the way she was still, listening, waiting. Nora was the best reporter on the paper for a reason: She was good at finding a story and researching every aspect of it. Unfortunately most of her articles were also really boring—like anyone wanted "An In-Depth History of Snow Valley's Student Government Voting Record"—but he knew quality work when he saw it.

And he could tell that Nora sensed some truth in what Henry had said about him.

Jack nodded, hoping to make it seem like no big deal. He probably wasn't pulling it off though—Jack wasn't good at faking things. Hiding things, yes, but not faking them. "Sasha and I have argued about some stuff. But it's not related to her locker or her bag or anything." His arguments with Sasha weren't something he felt like discussing—they made him angry.

Nora leaned forward slightly, her back straight, and Jack had a sudden urge to grab a pencil to capture the intensity of her gaze and posture, the way her normally pale cheeks were tinged with strawberry. He had only recently begun doing portraits and was discovering he quite enjoyed them. His sketch pad was in his bag and he pulled it out, then rooted around for a pencil. He decided sketching Nora, which would involve staring at her, would be creepy, but he knew he'd feel better drawing, so he began outlining Maddie's pink messenger bag, which was on the table in front of her.

But when he looked back up, realizing the room was silent, he saw Henry was grinning knowingly. Jack had no urge to capture Henry in a drawing, though if he did he'd call it *Portrait of an Idiot*. "So what did you argue about?" Henry asked.

"None of your business," Jack snapped, pressing down hard on the pencil. Now the line was too thick.

Maddie rubbed her chin for a moment. "Jack, listen, Henry is being super annoying." Henry squawked at this but Maddie talked over him. "The thing is, we're all suspects here and I think we have to start being honest with each other so that those of us who are innocent can get back to their lives."

Since Jack was one of those innocent people, he could see what she was saying. Plus Nora was nodding, and if Nora thought it was a good idea, it probably was. And he wasn't the awful person in the story anyway—that title belonged to Sasha.

So Jack told the story in one long breath. "It started when we were all getting Covid vaccines and everyone came back to school, and then there was this one time we had to close because of a few last cases, and Sasha said it was my fault because I'm Asian." Jack was actually mixed—Dad was Vietnamese American, Mom was white—though it wasn't like Charlie Wen, whose parents had brought their family here from China ten years ago, was responsible for Covid either.

Nora drew a sharp breath but it was Maddie who spoke first. "That is both racist and ignorant," she said angrily. "Asian Americans had nothing to do with Covid."

Jack, who had shouted this at Sasha, nodded wearily. There'd been a lot of racism and ignorance around Covid. Jack's dad, the celebrated Coach Tran, who had brought the Cougars, Allen University's baseball team, to five College World Series victories in ten years, had written an op-ed for the local paper about it after a microaggression appeared in the comments on the team blog. Even Matt, Jack's older brother and record-breaking SVSS baseball star, had dealt with some racist remarks.

Jack rubbed his soft eraser on his paper, then redrew the line.

"People like to find a scapegoat when something bad happens—" Nora began, but Henry cut her off.

"Why is it called a scapegoat and not a scape sheep? Do goats get blamed for things more than sheep?"

Nora's only indication of irritation was that she closed her eyes for an extra-long moment. "I don't think the saying is based on animal behavior. But my point is that Sasha scapegoating Jack like that is—"

"It could be though," Henry said, twirling on his chair. "I mean, do you really know about goat interaction?"

Nora turned so that her back faced Henry. "Jack, I can see why you fought with Sasha, and you were right to tell her off."

Jack's shoulders relaxed at this and he nodded as he began filling in details of Maddie's bag. "I don't like her but I wouldn't break into her locker or steal from her to let her know it. She knows."

Henry snickered appreciatively at this. Jack would have grinned at him if he liked Henry. But spending this much time together was proving what Jack could have guessed: He didn't really care for Henry.

"So then why were you here this morning?" Henry asked him, brushing his messy hair out of his eyes.

It was official: Jack completely disliked Henry. And there was no way he was telling any of them why he'd come in early. "Why were *you* here?" he countered. "And why am I the only one being honest about stuff? It's you guys' turn to start talking." He paused his drawing to glare at each of them.

Maddie was looking down at her nails, rubbing one finger over the polish. It was a light pink—actually, a blush, Jack decided. Henry was now rolling his chair around the front of the room. Neither seemed eager to speak up.

After a long silence, Nora leaned forward, her fingers knit together on the table in front of her. "I was here early because I had some things to do at the paper," she said.

Right, of course she did.

"Do you write for the paper?" Henry asked, sounding genuinely curious.

Jack could not bear to look at Nora to see her reaction. He knew she poured everything she had into her articles, and it had to feel bad that Henry didn't even know she worked on the paper. Nora's articles always had the least number of views and likes, but still. Jack himself got all kinds of likes for his drawings and occasional comics, which sometimes made him feel smug, but not now. Not when Nora worked so hard.

"Your article on Lane Animal Sanctuary was really good, Nora," Maddie said quickly. She smiled at Nora, and Jack realized Maddie, despite her status at school, was kind. Not everyone with power misused it like Sasha.

Nora smiled weakly and Jack now remembered that Nora had written about the local sanctuary over a year ago.

"We adopted our dog from there—she's the family baby," Maddie went on. "And totally spoiled."

Jack was liking Maddie more and more. "We adopted our cat, Dominic, from there too," Jack said, shading in the bag's strap. "And he's the best." Since Jack's family was two hard-core jocks and Jack (Mom had died seven years ago), Dad ran things a bit like a boot camp. Dominic had fit right in, standing expectantly in front of his food bowl at mealtimes and patting Jack's face with a paw if he overslept by more than thirty seconds. Dominic also loved to sleep at Jack's feet while Jack painted or drew when no one else was home, and at night he curled up, soft and warm, at Jack's side, his purr lulling Jack to sleep.

"I wish we had a pet," Henry said, more to himself than anyone else.

Jack wondered why they didn't just visit the sanctuary like so many other people in town.

"The only thing I read in the paper is Astrid's column," Henry said, loudly this time. He was pushing his chair around the table now, and Jack wanted to reach out and pinch him as he went by—yes, everyone read Astrid, but why mention that to Nora, the least-read writer on the paper?

"I adore Astrid," Maddie said, her eyes bright. "I wrote her about a problem I was having, and her advice was spot-on."

Henry was nodding and grinning. "Astrid is always spot-on," he said. "And her takedowns are the best."

Honest Astrid's Advice on Everything was hands down the most popular thing in the *Sentinel*. It was what Ms. Holt called a "cheeky" advice column, with clever solutions and snappy one-liners that made Jack laugh out loud. Plus it was where Jack's art got the most likes—because everyone loved Astrid.

Everyone but Nora. Nora was all about serious journalism and had complained more than once that Astrid brought down the IQ of the paper.

"Do you guys know who Astrid is?" Maddie asked.

Nora rolled her eyes and muttered, "Who cares," and Jack just shrugged. The general consensus of the *Sentinel* staff was that an anonymous high school student wrote Astrid—someone smart enough to have advice for all occasions and cool enough to make that advice fun. It was also generally agreed to let readers wonder—it gave the column even more mystique.

Jack glanced at the clock. "We don't have much time before Principal Montenegro comes back," he said, his shoulders squeezing up again. "Can someone please just confess and let the rest of us go already?"

Silence.

Finally Maddie spoke. "Okay, well, I'm here because Coach Faizal thought I came in last on the final drill at dance team practice, and whoever comes in last has to stay after practice and write up an official report of the day's workout on the clipboard. But I didn't feel like doing it then and I didn't have time yesterday—I came in right at seven this morning to do it. But the practice room was locked, so if I ever get out of this room, I'm going to be in big trouble with Coach Faizal. And I'm already pretty much her least favorite person on the team as it is."

"Because you're the worst dancer and that's why you came in last?" Henry asked cheerfully. He was coasting around the room, and when he passed Maddie, she reached out a foot and kicked his chair. It zoomed forward and rammed into the garbage can, causing Henry to yelp, which Jack had to admit he found pretty satisfying.

"No, actually, I didn't come in last. Lena did. But when I told the coach, she told me not to be a sore loser. And I might have argued," Maddie said, her words clipped. She was clearly still angry about the whole thing.

Jack glanced up from his drawing to give her a sympathetic look. "Lena didn't have your back?" he asked.

"She tried, but Coach Faizal says she calls it and that's that," Maddie said bitterly. Her red-gold hair was back in a ponytail she was twisting up tight around her fingers. "But anyway, that's why I was here this morning. I don't like Sasha either—she's an awful teammate on dance—super competitive and bossy. But I had no reason to break into her locker, and I definitely wouldn't take her backpack. She's always boasting about how it's designer—anyone who takes that is asking for a problem. And that's not me."

This all made sense. And even Jack had heard Sasha talk about the pack—whoever had taken it really *was* asking for a problem. Or clearly had a problem with Sasha, to want to make her angry like that.

"Hey, that is really realistic," Henry said, so close to Jack that Jack could feel Henry's breath on the back of his neck. *Creepy.* Jack jerked away as Henry moved even closer to Jack's drawing of Maddie's bag.

Maddie peered over. "Wow, that is for real good—I can't believe you did it in, like, ten minutes."

Jack could not help grinning at this.

"You are seriously talented," Henry said cheerfully, sitting back down in his chair to roll around the table again.

"Half of the student art display is Jack's stuff," Nora said. She smiled at Jack, but his chest filled with rocks at her words.

"Cool," Maddie said, letting her ponytail fall free. "I'm not in the Gala this year because I didn't make the squad for the dance team's big finale."

"Because you're the worst dancer, we remember," Henry said. He had gotten stuck between two chairs and was backing up.

Maddie glared but then couldn't help laughing. "No, because only four middle schoolers got picked for the squad—Emma, Jade, Kiara, and Lena. This is a big showcase since it's going to be livestreamed on Tansy Mink's YouTube channel, which you probably never heard of, but if you danced, you'd know it. She has over ten million followers. Everyone in the school dance scene will be watching, all over the country. So only our best dancers made it. But that doesn't make me the worst."

Maddie seemed fine with this, which was kind of surprising. Though maybe she was just happy to be on the team and didn't need to be part of the big Starlight finale.

"Your family must be so proud that you're the star of the art display," Maddie added, turning back to Jack.

For a moment Jack was unable to speak, but he knew he had to. It was time to say why he'd come in early and prove that he, like Maddie and Nora, was innocent. Otherwise who knew how long they'd be stuck in room 122? So Jack took a deep breath and spilled the truth.

"Actually," he said, "they're not."

CHAPTER 3

HENRY

Henry had managed to back the chair up and was now coasting along the side of the table where Jack was sitting. Jack kept glaring at him, but Henry couldn't stop—he was too jittery to stay still.

He was interested in what Jack would say, of course. How could Jack not be excited for his parents and any siblings to see how great he was? They probably knew but still, parents loved seeing their kids celebrated at school. Not that Henry knew this from personal experience. But on TV parents always went nuts when their kid got elected class president or whatever. Plus Jack's stuff was so good it could be in a museum—his parents had to be thrilled about that.

"My dad and brother are super into baseball," Jack began.

"Duh," Henry could not help interrupting. Because what person with a brain did not know that? Coach Tran was on TV and in the paper all the time. Real

TV, like ESPN, because that's how good his coaching skills were. And Matt was the best player to ever play for SVSS. It wasn't even close. Matt was so good, he'd been on ESPN too.

Maddie sent Henry a death glare. "Let him talk," she hissed.

Whatever. Henry would let Jack continue, but if he said something that obvious again, Henry made no promises he could keep quiet.

"But so yeah, my family's all about baseball, all the time," Jack went on, looking only at Nora and Maddie.

Henry didn't want to interrupt again but he had no choice—he had a question.

"What about your mom?" he asked, cruising around the corner of the table. He was getting quite good at driving his chair.

"Shut up," Nora snapped. Henry didn't know Nora well, but even he could tell this was a big reaction from her. So *now* what had he done?

"It's fine," Jack said with a sigh. "First of all, my mom was baseball crazy too—she was a softball pitcher in college and brought her team to the College World Series twice."

A weight had settled on Henry's shoulders when

Jack said "was," and it pressed down harder as Jack went on.

"She was a coach at Allen University, like my dad, but she died of cancer seven years ago."

"Sorry," Henry mumbled as a wheel from his chair caught on the leg of the table.

"But anyway, my dad and my brother are waiting for me to get into baseball. Which is not going to happen"—he glanced at Henry as if he could tell Henry was about to interrupt again—"because I don't like it and I'm not good at it and all I want is to be an artist."

Jack was back to drawing, moving his pencil forcefully along the paper. "I came in this morning to try and take my stuff down from the Starlight display. I don't want to have to talk to them about my art at some big public school event. Especially one where Dad is a VIP. The baseball team is going to have a photo op with him after they do their demo," he explained.

Nora and Maddie began saying things about how art was as important as baseball, about how Jack's family should respect him, and Henry agreed with all of it. But he was too worried about what was next to bother joining in—not that Jack would care what he thought anyway. But Henry had bigger problems: It was his turn. Everyone had said why they were there this morning and why they might not get along with Sasha (well, Nora hadn't said anything about not liking Sasha, but if she did, her reason would be something goody-goody, like Sasha didn't do her part in group work or something. Not like Henry. Nothing like Henry).

Which was all to say it seemed like a good time to leave.

"Going to the bathroom," Henry announced, jumping off his chair and bounding for the door.

"Wait," he heard Maddie call as he let the door close behind him. He jogged down the hall in case they tried to open the door to shout after him, but slowed when he rounded the corner. He didn't need to get caught running in the halls—he was in enough of a mess as it was, and the last thing he needed was his parents getting called.

Henry shook this fear from his head and focused. It was hard to think in room 122, where it took all his brainpower to appear like he couldn't care less he was serving an in-school suspension. Because the thing he could not—would not—explain was why he desperately disliked Sasha Saturday. It would make him look like he'd have reason to do something like break into her locker. He hadn't. Obviously. If he ever messed with Sasha, she would use what she had on him to retaliate, and then—well, Henry wasn't going to think about that. The point was, if he could distract them by doing what he always did—act like nothing mattered to him—he'd stay safe. Hopefully.

After another minute of pacing the halls, Henry decided it would be okay to tell the other three why he was here this morning—or part of it. Henry had been in the library and could prove it with the granola bar wrapper stuffed in his pocket. Ms. MacCullough kept snacks on hand because she said it was impossible to enjoy a good book on an empty stomach. As long as they didn't press him about *why* he was there—or his issues with Sasha—he'd be okay.

But just then the door to room 140 opened, and as though she'd been summoned from his deepest fears, out pranced Sasha Saturday.

"Henry, I thought I saw you passing by," she said.

Henry stood, blinking, a deer in headlights, waiting for the hit to come. Because it was coming.

"I hear you, Maddie, Jack, and Nora are the ones

who broke into my locker," she said evenly. "Or one of you did—but until I know who, you're all guilty in my book."

"I didn't do it," Henry managed to croak.

Sasha smiled, her eyes glittering coldly, like an alligator about to take out a family of ducklings.

"You know what I'll have to reveal to the school if it was you," she said. "I'd rather not share that information, obviously. I'd planned to keep it to myself. I know how it would upset you for everyone to find out. But if you give me no choice . . ."

She let her voice drift off, her meaning clear. "Please let the others know I'll be revealing things about them as well, should the need arise."

Henry nodded, his voice smothered somewhere deep in his throat.

Sasha leaned forward. She was both taller and more athletic than Henry and he stepped back instinctively. "I want to know who did this and I want my stuff," she said, biting down on each word. "Make it happen and make it happen fast."

Henry practically tripped over his own feet racing back to room 122. He needed answers. And he needed them fast.

"Henry, you—" Maddie began, but when Henry shut the door tight and leaned against it, she stopped. "Um, are you okay?"

"I just saw Sasha," he said. "She wants her bag back, like, yesterday and she's threatening us to make it happen."

Jack frowned. "Threatening us how?"

Henry took a moment to make it come out right because his heart was actually hurting his chest it was thumping so hard, and that made it difficult to talk. "I don't like Sasha but I would never break into her locker, for the same reason we have to get her that bag back—she's threatening to tell something she knows about me—and she said she'll reveal something about you guys too. Something bad."

Maddie shook her head. "She doesn't know anything about me." Her phone dinged and she looked down, then tapped open the message, which frustrated Henry even more. This was not the time to be distracted. This was the time to act!

"That's not the point!" he snarled. "The point is, we're in trouble and we're only going to be in more trouble if we don't get her that stupid backpack!"

Nora leaned forward, her gaze intense as she stared

at Henry. "Let's start here: What were you doing here this morning?"

That was fair—everyone else had already shared this after all.

"I was in the library and I have a granola bar wrapper to prove it," Henry said. His hands were shaking as he took the slick scrap of foil out of his pocket.

Nora nodded and sat back. "Okay, well, then this is the problem," she said. "I don't think anyone in this room took Sasha's backpack."

Henry was about to protest when he realized something: Nora was right. After they'd spent nearly thirty minutes locked up together, one thing seemed pretty clear—none of them had broken into Sasha's locker and taken her backpack.

CHAPTER 4

MADDIE

Maddie was gazing down at her phone, unable to believe what she was seeing. Even though she had played it three times. On mute, obviously. She didn't need the volume to know what was being said. What she, herself, had said in the locker room after Coach Faizal called her out as last in the dance drill. Maddie had said quite a lot as she pulled her things from her locker, all of it ripping apart Coach Faizal, and all of it captured on video. By Sasha. There was no note to go along with the video, but Henry had made Sasha's message clear. She would show Coach what Maddie had said if her stupid fancy backpack wasn't returned.

So Sasha *did* know something about Maddie, and it was truly bad.

Until now, Maddie didn't care too much who had done it—she just wanted to get to class. But now she *had* to get Sasha her pack back.

The other three were silent, taking in what Nora had just said.

"So if none of us did it, who did?" Maddie asked, stuffing her phone in her bag like it had scalded her. Which it kind of had.

Before anyone could respond, the door opened, shoving Henry, who was still leaning on it, to the side as Principal Montenegro strode in.

"Who's ready to confess?" she demanded, staring at each of them.

Maddie did her best not to flinch when her eyes met the principal's, but it was hard—Principal Montenegro had a vaporizing glare. That was not something Maddie had been previously aware of. She'd never been in trouble beyond occasionally running late for class, and most people in school gave dance team members a break. Maddie wasn't sure this was fair, especially since some of the girls, like Sasha, took advantage of it. But she herself was not above being allowed to enter a class without a late pass or not being scolded for talking to a friend after the bell rang. Clearly though, there was no free pass when the principal thought you might have committed an actual crime. *This* was what it felt like to be in trouble.

"The thing is," Jack said, his hands clenched in front of him, "none of us did it. We all had reasons—"

Principal Montenegro slammed a hand down on the table so hard all four of them jumped. "I do not want to hear it," she said through gritted teeth. "The Saturdays' lawyer will step in if the school can't solve this, with an investigator, and I think it's safe to say we would all prefer that not to happen."

Maddie's heart nearly stopped at this statement, because yeah, they did not want that.

"Why is a stolen backpack such a big deal?" Henry asked. He said it so timidly Maddie could tell he knew it was a bad idea to speak, but couldn't help himself. And it kind of *was* a good question.

"Because it is a valuable bag," Principal Montenegro said with a sigh. "And normally an item left overnight is the student's responsibility, but in this case it was the school's fault she was unable to retrieve it yesterday."

That was because one of the buses getting back from the extremely boring field trip to Lowden County History Museum had gotten a flat, which Maddie didn't even know could happen to such big tires. But by the time the seventh graders on that bus returned to school, it was locked and their parents were in the parking lot to take them home. Maddie's friend Jade had been on the bus, texting the whole saga to everyone on the dance team. So it *was* the school's fault Sasha's bag was taken. And clearly the lawyer was going to make it a problem for the principal if she couldn't uncover what had happened. And whoever had stolen that backpack? They were going down.

"You have thirty more minutes, and then we'll have to call the lawyer's office to let her know the guilty party has yet to be identified." With that Principal Montenegro swept out of the room.

"This is bad—" Jack said at the same time Henry said, "Are you sure none of you did it?"

Maddie noticed that he was looking right at Jack when he asked that.

"Why are you looking at me?" Jack asked in a very still voice.

"Because—" Henry began, but Nora stood up and interrupted him.

"We don't have time for this," she said firmly. Maddie was impressed by how firmly, actually. She didn't really know Nora, but clearly her reputation of being tough and serious was earned.

"None of us did it," Nora went on crisply. "No one

here is dumb enough to actually wait for a lawyer or investigator or whatever to come and find out they're guilty. Someone else did it and we have thirty minutes to find out who."

"So where do we start?" Jack asked. He was stuffing his sketch in his bag like it was just some doodle. Maddie couldn't believe his dad and brother weren't doing backflips of pride given how talented Jack was.

"We make a list of Sasha's enemies," Henry said decisively, tugging at his hair. "Then we go talk to them."

Maddie was unsure of who Henry had become in the past five minutes. She'd known Henry for years and all he did, especially after they'd all come back from the Covid closing, was joke around. He never took anything seriously, ever. Yet in the past few minutes he'd yelled about Sasha blackmailing them, and now he was actually offering a reasonable suggestion. It was as though this mattered to him—a lot.

Which made Maddie extremely curious: What exactly did Sasha have on Henry?

"That could work," Jack said, sounding reluctant to agree with Henry.

"With some people it would be a good place to

start," Nora said authoritatively. "But Sasha has so many enemies we'd be here all day just writing them down—I mean, even right here, all four of us have reason to dislike her because she just threatened us."

Maddie noted that Nora did not say Sasha was lying. Was it possible Sasha really did know something less than perfect about Nora?

"Okay, well, on crime shows they investigate the scene of the crime and then take pictures and study them for clues," Henry announced. "We should do that. Starting with Sasha's locker."

"Wait, you mean leave this room? Principal Montenegro said we had to stay here," Maddie said.

"It's that or we're all under investigation and maybe even locked up until we confess," Henry said. "And there's no time to waste."

Maddie thought that was probably an exaggeration (she hoped so anyway), but he had a point. Two points actually: The clock was ticking down and they had exactly twenty-six minutes to get this done.

"I don't think we can worry about getting caught sneaking around school when our other option is dealing with a lawyer," Jack agreed. "But let's not get caught."

"Good plan," Henry said, grinning.

Jack did not grin back but he was standing up.

Maddie looked at Nora, who was rising as well. So even she thought this was a good idea.

"Do we really need to take pictures?" Jack asked. "It's not like we'll be able to see much on our phones—they're too small. On cop shows they blow them up and stuff."

That was a good point.

"I have a photographic memory anyway," Nora said, putting her odd-looking leather bag thing in her seat.

"That's real?" Henry asked. "I thought it was a made-up superpower, like being able to time travel."

Maddie couldn't help laughing a little at that, but Nora just nodded. She was walking toward the door, and as she passed Maddie, Maddie noticed how short she was. Nora seemed like she should be taller than Maddie—taller than everyone in the room. But she was actually a "bit of a petite thing," as Maddie's stepmother, Charlotte, would say.

"Yeah, I remember all the details of what I read or observe," Nora said matter-of-factly.

Of course she did. When brains were handed

out, Nora had obviously gotten the supersonic kind. Not that Maddie had issues about her own smarts—especially when it came to math. But still, a photographic memory sounded cool.

Maddie put her own, non-designer bag on her seat, wondering if it would be weird to ask Jack for his sketch of it. Which was a random thought, but this was what happened to Maddie when she was anxious: She had a lot of random thoughts.

"Hurry, you guys," Jack said, heading for the door. "We don't have time to mess around."

"So we're really leaving in-school suspension to go search for clues?" Maddie asked, gripping her messenger bag.

"Yeah," said the new Henry, opening the door. "We are."

Nora and Jack were on his heels, so Maddie released her bag and, with one last glance behind her, followed.

CHAPTER 5

HENRY

Henry's shoulders hadn't unclenched since the awful run-in with Sasha, but being out in the hall, actually doing something, helped. At least a little. He still couldn't believe it was on them to find out who had broken into the locker.

They went the long way around, to avoid passing the main office. Maddie was glancing anxiously behind them while Jack was practically tiptoeing. Nora, meanwhile, was gesturing that they should duck down at class doors so no one inside could see them. Which Henry should have done before, to avoid seeing Sasha. Though maybe best to know what she was planning—on his favorite show the detective always tried to gather all the information possible to know what he was up against.

Jack, who was in the lead, slowed as they reached the corner and then peered quickly around.

"It's all clear," he whispered, and the four of them

walked down the hall where the A locker alcove was located. None of them had needed to ask where Sasha's locker was because everyone had seen her holding court there on a regular basis. And who hadn't noticed the balloons and cards that had spilled out of the alcove on her birthday a few weeks ago? At the time Henry had been mystified that so many people wanted to celebrate Sasha to such lengths. But maybe some of them were hoping that gifting Sasha with balloons or a teddy bear would mean she'd be nicer to them. Now Henry was thinking he should have bought her something too.

Jack went ahead to peek around all corners of the alcove while Nora strode up to the locker, which was surrounded by cones. Henry had half expected the whole area to be cordoned off with police tape, which would have been kind of cool. The cones were just kind of annoyingly in the way.

"Okay, let's do this," Jack said quietly, coming back around to where Henry, Nora, and Maddie were waiting. Henry noticed Jack only looked at the girls and not him. Not that Henry cared. But it *was* rude.

Nora and Maddie peered at the locker door while Jack crouched down to see if any clues might have fallen on the floor. Henry decided to check the hall, in case something incriminating might have been dropped and then kicked out in the morning rush, but as he turned, he tripped over the plastic recycling bin and fell into the garbage can right next to it.

"Careful!" Maddie whispered at the same time Jack hissed, "Be quiet."

Henry's face warmed as he stood up. TV detectives never tripped like that. "Those bins aren't usually so close to the alcove," he said.

The garbage and recycling were always outside the locker alcoves, not practically inside. Someone had obviously moved them, and Henry did not appreciate it.

"Right," Jack scoffed quietly. He always seemed happy to have an excuse to mock Henry.

Before today Jack had seemed like a nice guy, but not anymore.

"What are we looking for here?" Maddie asked, turning to them. "Because all I see is a locker."

"Something suspicious or out of place," Nora said, shaking her head. "But there isn't anything."

This was a setback for sure, but Henry reassured

himself that setbacks were part of the process; anyone who watched a detective show knew that.

"Is there anywhere else we can look?" Maddie asked. She glanced at the clock on the wall behind him. "And fast?"

There was a short silence. Henry, who did not want to know how little time they had left, was thinking about what his favorite detective, Columbo, would do. The answer, he decided, was to brainstorm possibilities. "What do we know about the suspect?" he asked.

"They wanted something from Sasha's locker?" Jack asked in a sarcastic voice.

Jack was not good at brainstorming.

"Well, they came into school early," Maddie said gamely, which Henry appreciated.

"Couldn't they have broken into her locker last night?" Jack asked, flexing his fingers. Henry wondered if artists did finger exercises like athletes did whole-body exercises, to build muscle.

"No," Maddie said, shaking her head. "Remember how Principal Montenegro said last night everything was fine when Mr. Smith locked up and left? Whoever broke in had to have done it this morning."

"And the only ones caught on the video foot-age from the front door were us," Henry exclaimed. "Which means—"

Nora had lit up. "It means they figured out how to get into school without walking through the front entrance!"

"There's no footage from the video cameras at the other doors?" Jack asked.

"No," Henry said triumphantly. "Those cameras don't go on until those doors open, at seven forty-five."

"So whoever we're looking for knew that and knew how to avoid being detected," Maddie said.

"Right," Henry said, all fired up at this new lead. "So let's go check out the other doors and see how they did it."

Even Jack was nodding at this.

This time it was Henry who peered around the side of the alcove to make sure the coast was clear, then hurried out, leading them to the exit by the gym.

This was thwarted by the fact that there was a class inside.

"Maybe we should—" Henry began, but then the bell rang, nearly giving Henry a heart attack. His first instinct was to run, but then he realized first period ending was actually a terrific stroke of luck.

Jack looked frozen in place and Maddie was glancing around, panicked. But Nora was watching Henry closely and started to smile.

"Great," she said cheerfully. Maddie and Jack looked at her like she'd lost it.

"We're going to get caught," Jack said tersely, "and that is very *not* great."

"Not if we keep a low profile and avoid the main office," Nora said, shaking her head. "If we do that, then this is four minutes we don't have to sneak around—we can blend in and act like we're heading to class."

"Oh yeah," Maddie said with a loud exhale.

"Smart," Jack said to Nora, his voice normal again.

Henry wished he'd been the one to point it out, but whatever.

"We can check out the gym exit while we're here," he said. Because the faster they could cover things, the better.

"Right," Nora said, starting toward it. But then she stopped. "I have no reason to be in the gym. We need to have an excuse if one of the gym teachers comes in to prepare for next period."

That was wise. The gym teachers generally waited for classes outside the locker room area but could certainly step into the gym and catch Nora there.

"I've got this," Maddie said confidently, striding through the metal doors. Henry realized that of course, as a member of the dance team, she could say she was looking for the dance team coach.

"So what's the detective show you watch?" Nora asked as sixth graders streamed past for gym class.

"It's called *Columbo*," Henry said. It was strange to be surrounded by voices and people after being locked in the small classroom with Maddie, Nora, and Jack. Actually it was probably a regular-sized classroom, but it felt like the walls had been closing in around them.

Jack frowned. "I've never heard of it." He knelt down to tie his shoe, and Henry noticed his sneakers were new.

"It's an old show, right?" Nora said. "I think my grandma likes it—she watches it on cable because it's not streaming anywhere."

Jack scoffed at this and Henry stiffened.

But Nora was already giving Jack an arch look. "I'll

have you know my grandmother is extremely sophisticated in her taste."

Henry stifled a snicker at Jack's face as Nora turned to Henry. "I think it's cool you like old shows. Did you ever see *L.A. Law*? I think that's the one my grandma watches after *Columbo*."

"Once or twice," Henry lied, not quite looking at Nora. He did not watch *Columbo* on cable because his family did not have cable. Or any streaming services. They just had an old DVD player and a bunch of shows on disc that his parents had collected.

Luckily Maddie was walking back.

"Hey, Maddie," an eighth-grade girl walking past called. "See you this afternoon."

"Yup," Maddie said, waving to her friends as she came up next to Nora. "I hope Coach goes a little easier on us today."

"Good luck with that," the girl said, and they both laughed.

It would be fun to be part of some kind of team. Henry went home every day after school to take care of his younger siblings, Lacey and George. Which was fun too. They made blanket forts and ate peanut butter from the jar, and on nice days Henry took them out back to play "The Scary Monster Is Coming," which was a hybrid of tag and hide-and-seek. But it would be kind of cool to hang out with people his age sometimes too, doing something together that wasn't a stupid group project or whatever. His friends Lena and Nathan came over sometimes, but Lena was busy with dance team now and Nathan played soccer. And Henry knew hanging out with a six- and eight-year-old who tried to get peanut butter in your hair wasn't how most people wanted to spend time.

"The gym exit door has an alarm," Maddie said under her breath. "There's no way our culprit could have gotten in that way."

Henry appreciated her detective lingo. He should have thought to use the word *culprit*.

"Let's try the exit by the library," Nora suggested. She took off, moving surprisingly quickly for someone so small.

The halls were emptying out—the bell for second period was going to ring in less than a minute. The four of them hurried past the auditorium and a row of classrooms. The bell rang just as they reached the next exit. There was no alarm on this one.

Henry knelt to see if the culprit may have dropped

something incriminating while Maddie ran a hand over the doorjamb and Nora scanned the walls on both sides. But nothing was amiss.

"I'm going to open the door," Jack announced. "Maybe the culprit left a stolen key or something to pick the lock."

But they did not have to look outside to see how the culprit had gotten in: The lockset had been carefully taped over and the door slid open easily.

"So if someone planned this theft in advance, they could have put this on yesterday at the end of school. That way, the door wouldn't have locked last night," Nora said, running a finger over the tape. "Which means they could have snuck in early this morning and totally avoided the cameras."

Nora was spot-on.

"Another dead end," Maddie said with a sigh.

"Not necessarily," Henry said, thinking like Columbo. "We've learned a lot. This was carefully planned and that tells us psychological traits of whoever stole the backpack. I mean, they took the time to do research on how to prop open a door without any external evidence."

Henry was pleased he'd used such a technical term,

and Nora was nodding. "And they knew the camera schedule—that they could sneak in here undetected if they came in early enough."

That was a great point.

"Maybe they work in the office," Jack said. "A student volunteer would know something like that."

Another great point—the profile was beginning to take shape.

"Where to next?" Maddie asked, looking at Henry.

Henry wasn't sure. What would Columbo do with the start of a suspect profile and the clock ticking down?

"Um, maybe we should go back to the classroom and brainstorm more," Henry said.

Maddie looked unimpressed by this answer, and who could blame her? But standing around the hall trying to figure it out obviously wasn't smart. So the four of them headed back to room 122.

"I'm just going to grab some more pencils from my locker," Jack said, stopping at the D alcove.

"What do you need a pencil for?" Henry asked, irritated. It wasn't like Jack had to take notes.

"For sketching," Jack informed him in an icy tone. "I think better when I draw. I'll meet you guys there in a minute."

Normally Henry would find a way to make a joke about this statement, but right now he was too tense, so he just continued toward the classroom. If pencils would make Jack better at brainstorming, that was fine. Jack not being in the room, hating Henry, was also fine. What *wasn't* fine was that they hadn't identified the culprit yet.

Once inside, Henry headed over to his chair, ready to start driving it around the room to release the jitteriness trapped in his limbs. But then Maddie sucked in a breath so loudly Henry could hear it whistling into her lungs.

"You guys," she said, her voice quaking. "We are running out of time."

Henry looked at the clock, and now his whole body started to tremble. Because Maddie was right: They had twelve minutes left to figure out who had broken into Sasha's locker before Principal Montenegro returned.

CHAPTER 6

JACK

"Hello, Jack."

Jack was just shutting his locker when Sasha's voice, velvet and laced with poison, made him jump.

Jack spun around and glared at the person he most disliked at Snow Valley Secondary.

"Happy to see me," Sasha said, grinning like the viper she was. "I love that." She smoothed a lock of shiny chestnut hair back from her face, which glowed a golden pink, her big blue eyes wide. Even if her hair was dyed and her glow came from makeup, her features and colors were striking. But something Jack had begun learning doing portraits was that much of what made a person beautiful to behold was the personality shining through in their features. That was what an artist tried to capture. And the reason Jack would never want to draw Sasha, who was still gazing at him intently. Because there was no authentic beauty there, at least not that Jack had ever seen.

54

Jack rolled his eyes and started out of the locker area.

"You can ignore me, that's fine," Sasha said, following him out. "But know this: If you took my stuff, you'll pay. Or more accurately, your brother will pay."

Jack dropped the pencils in his hand and they fell to the floor, scattering. *This* was what Sasha had over him? "Good, you know the secret I'm referring to, so we understand each other," Sasha said, walking by Jack and stepping on one of the pencils, cracking it in half as she headed back to her lair.

Jack was shaking with fury as he knelt down to pick up his pencils. They were not regular pencils but the expensive kind used for art. He clenched a fist around the pieces of the one Sasha had destroyed, its edges sharp against his skin, but nowhere near as painful as Sasha's words. Her *threats*. His heart was thumping extra hard in his chest as he strode back to room 122, and his body was uncomfortably overheated, like he'd stepped into an oven. That she would threaten Matt like that—it was despicable. Disgusting. Utterly and completely appalling.

But most of all it was terrifying. He had no idea how she'd discovered it, but they both knew what she had found out and they both knew that it was information Matt hoped to keep private for right now. Until he was ready to share it on his terms. Sasha exposing it before then, in a way that would be as gross and awful as possible—Jack was sure of that—would hurt Matt. And there was no way Jack could allow that. Sure, Matt gave him a hard time about baseball. But Matt protected him, loved him without question, and had his back no matter what. There was no way Jack could let him down. No way at all.

Jack shoved open the door to room 122 and was infuriated when he saw that the other three were sitting around the table doing absolutely nothing.

"What's the plan?" he snapped, stalking inside.

"We're working on that," Maddie said, raising a brow at his tone.

"We need to work faster," Jack growled.

Nora was looking at him carefully. "I'm guessing you ran into Sasha?"

Nora was scary smart. Jack nodded and the three of them looked instantly sympathetic. Which was nice and all, but with ten minutes left, not helpful. Not with what was on the line.

"Maybe we should figure out all the students who

volunteer in the office," Henry said, spinning around in his chair. "And then try to talk to them. Fast."

Like Jack was interested in Henry's ideas! Henry had basically accused Jack of being the one to break into Sasha's locker and lie about it, until Nora pointed out that none of them would be that stupid. Plus, where had Henry's brilliant ideas gotten them so far? Okay, maybe they had a few clues, but so what? They didn't have the culprit and that was what they needed. So Jack was done listening to Henry.

"Does anyone who actually knows anything have a plan?" Jack asked, looking pointedly at Nora and Maddie. He slapped his whole pencils down on the table (but not too hard—he didn't want to break more of them) for emphasis.

"What's your problem?" Henry demanded, walking over to Jack. He was Jack's height, so Jack stared directly into his eyes, seething. Henry seemed to be seething himself. But whatever dumb secret Henry thought he had to protect, it was nothing compared with Jack's burning need to protect his brother.

"If you guys actually fight, I'm going to kill you both," Maddie said with a sigh. "And thinking about who works in the office is a good idea."

"You're wasting time we don't have," Nora added, raising a brow. "Back off and let's make a list of office volunteers."

This was fine with Jack. He'd never actually been in a fight, and contrary to some of the idiotic questions he got, not every Asian knew martial arts. He wasn't scared of fighting so much as he was scared of damaging one of his hands in a bad punch attempt. Well, actually he was scared of fighting too, but he wasn't going to admit that. He just glared a little harder at Henry, then walked over to the garbage and tossed in the pieces of the pencil Sasha had ruined. They hit the bottom of the metal can with a clank, and Jack could not resist one more dig at Henry.

"Careful, you don't want to trip over that one too," he said with a smirk.

Henry gave Jack a withering glare. "The garbage didn't belong so close to the alcove," he said, with some bite. "I don't know who—"

He stopped talking and pressed his hands against his head, like he'd just come up with something brilliant. "The garbage!"

Jack stepped back, unsure of what was happening.

"It was moved!" Henry shouted.

Jack glanced at Maddie and Nora, who both looked as perplexed as he felt.

"The garbage is part of the crime scene!" Henry said, bouncing toward the door. "That's why it got moved—someone used it early this morning and didn't want anyone to see what they were throwing away. And that someone may have been the culprit!"

"Henry, you're brilliant!" Nora practically squealed, rushing to catch up with Henry, who was looking out in the hall, then wrenching open the door. The two of them raced out.

Maddie turned to Jack. "Do we know what is happening?" she asked.

Jack shook his head. "No, we do not. But I guess we should go with them. They seem pretty excited."

Maddie snickered. "That's an understatement."

And so the two of them took off.

But as they caught up to Nora and Henry, who were about to fly around the corner, they both came to an abrupt halt. Jack nearly slammed into Henry, and was about to make a fuss, when he heard it too: voices and footsteps. Footsteps that were coming closer.

Maddie's face was turning an alarming shade of gray, and she pressed her hands over her mouth. Jack could feel his heart starting to slam against his rib cage. He looked around frantically for an escape. But the classrooms around them were full. Jack's stomach curdled, his mouth suddenly dry. If whoever this was turned the corner, they'd walk right into them. But even if they kept going straight down the other hall, one glance their way and they'd be done for.

Unlike the rest of them, Henry was calm as he gestured that they should flatten against the wall. Which was ridiculous and something he'd probably seen on TV and would obviously never work. But it was also the only option, so Jack pressed his back against the cool of the wall, making himself as two-dimensional as possible. And then he held his breath.

". . . and the PTA was certainly upset about it." Jack closed his eyes because the speaker was Mr. Jenkins, the science teacher, who was allergic to laughter and a zealous enforcer of rules. The smaller the rule, the more pleasure he got out of enforcing it. "She's off to a shaky start, that's for sure." The other teacher was Ms. Kingston, who taught eighth-grade health, a class Jack was not looking forward to. "And angering the PTA so early in her tenure when they were iffy about her replacing Principal Grace last year—it makes me wonder how long she'll last."

Nora sucked in a breath and Jack realized they were talking about Ms. Montenegro. Apparently she had done something to upset the PTA—which was probably making her even more eager to get that backpack returned to Sasha, since Sasha's mom was PTA president.

This was not good news—what if she was determined to blame someone and wouldn't listen to them when they said they were innocent?

A moment later the teachers had passed, never looking around the corner to see four seventh graders pressed against the wall.

They waited until the two voices faded and then detached themselves. Jack's T-shirt was damp from panic sweat that had beaded down his back. It was gross but at least they hadn't gotten caught.

"Come on," Henry whispered, taking off again before Jack could ask why they were running all over the place, risking getting caught by another teacher.

When they reached Henry, he was rooting through the garbage can right by the A locker alcove.

"Ohh, the culprit might have thrown away evidence!" Maddie said gleefully, clapping her hands.

"Evidence that might tell us more about who they are," Jack added, nodding and subtly trying to wipe the remaining sweat off his forehead.

They beamed at each other. Then Maddie turned to Henry. "Great idea to go two-dimensional so Mr. Jenkins wouldn't see us," she said.

"Yeah, it really was," Nora said admiringly. Which grated on Jack, even though it was true.

Especially because it was true.

"I wasn't sure it would work," Henry said, "but—" He stopped suddenly and jerked his arm out of the can.

The other three leaned forward, ready for answers. But instead Henry's hand came up coated with rotten banana.

"That is so gross," Maddie said, twirling away.

Nora frowned. "I hope that banana didn't ruin the evidence, if there is any."

"Thanks for your concern for my hand," Henry sniffed, and despite himself, Jack laughed. "Someone else can help now," Henry added as he walked over to the water fountain to clean off.

Nora pulled the plastic bag out of the garbage

can and set it on the floor. Maddie knelt down beside her and the two of them inspected the few contents through the safety of the clear plastic.

"You might have suggested that to me," Henry said sourly.

"Not so loud," Nora hissed.

Jack felt useless but then noticed the small blue container on the other side of the alcove. "I'll check the recycling," he announced.

"Does anyone really recycle?" Maddie asked skeptically. "Besides teachers?"

"I do," Nora said, sounding outraged.

Jack nodded. Recycling was important—Dad was vehement about it.

There were only a few pieces of paper in the bucket. He pulled them out and started going through each one. And at the third piece, he gasped.

"You guys," he said, "I think I found what we're looking for."

CHAPTER 7

MADDIE

"Okay, show us," Maddie demanded the moment the four of them arrived back at room 122. They'd realized that with less than five minutes until the return of Ms. Montenegro, it would be best to look at Jack's discovery in the room. But the wait had nearly killed Maddie.

Jack laid the paper on the table and the three of them crowded in to see over his shoulders, Nora squeezing around to be in the front. Maddie focused on what was written in hasty pencil on the basic lined piece of paper: two locker combinations and the morning schedule of which janitors and administrators typically passed locker alcove A and what time they passed.

"This is what the culprit used to sneak into the building, avoid being seen, and then break into Sasha's locker," Maddie breathed, unable to believe they had actually found this.

"Why are there *two* locker combinations?" Jack asked, stepping back.

This made Maddie pause—that part didn't make sense.

"Maybe the culprit didn't know which one it was," Nora said, still looking at the paper. "Maybe . . . they found a list of combinations that included Sasha's from this year and last year, so the culprit wrote them both down."

"This is amazing," Henry said, flopping into a chair. "But it's also worthless."

Jack was nodding. "Because we have no idea who wrote it."

This was true. Horribly, unfairly true. Maddie's eyes prickled and her throat was suddenly raw. She blinked and swallowed, not wanting to cry.

"Maybe we can do a handwriting test to prove it wasn't one of us," she said feebly, thudding down in the nearest chair. How could they have gotten this close, only to fail?

"Yeah, when the lawyer gets here," Henry said bitterly.

There was no way Maddie was keeping it together

if that happened. She had never imagined she'd be a suspect in something so serious that a lawyer might talk to her. She ducked her head and rubbed her eyes with the back of her hand, not wanting the others to see how upset she felt.

"I can't believe we found such an amazing piece of evidence but still don't know who broke into her locker," Jack said, kicking at his chair.

"Actually," Nora said slowly, looking at her fingers, which were laced together, "I can figure out who wrote this."

Maddie sat up as if zapped by an electric bolt because if Nora was right—

"How is that possible?" Henry asked.

"Does it have to do with your photographic memory?" Maddie asked. Because it *had* seemed almost like a superpower.

"Yeah," Nora said. "The writing looks familiar—I know I've seen it before, but I can't remember where. I think I can figure it out if we can narrow it down . . . What do we know about our culprit?"

"Okay," Maddie said, suddenly feeling more hopeful. She was confused but she trusted Nora. She cleared her throat before speaking again. "Well, the thief is someone who recycles."

Henry snickered and Jack made a strange noise, like he was trying *not* to snicker because he didn't want to laugh with Henry.

Boys were ridiculous sometimes.

"And they knew the janitor's morning schedule, so maybe they go to the library before school," Jack said.

Maddie nodded. It was a safe bet that Henry was not the only one who hung out there in the mornings. Everyone liked the library.

"This person does good research—they found out the camera schedule and figured out when the custodians are near the A alcove in the morning," Henry said. "And looked up how to prevent a door from locking."

"Remember, they might also be a volunteer at the office," Maddie added, twirling her ponytail.

"That's what I needed," Nora said, nodding. "I know who our culprit is."

Maddie was ready to cheer, but then she looked more closely at Nora. Instead of appearing triumphant, Nora's face was turning a blotchy pink and she was staring down at her hands.

"This is amazing!" Henry exclaimed, throwing out his arms. "Tell us everything!"

"Start at the beginning," Jack added, grinning as he leaned toward Nora. "How did you figure it out?"

Nora shook her head, her eyes still on her clenched hands. "I can't tell you," she practically whispered. "I can only tell you who did it. That's it."

That was *not* it—not if Maddie had anything to say about it!

"Of course you have to tell us!" Henry said, outraged, as if he'd never heard anything so absurd.

"Listen, Nora," Maddie said, keeping her voice calm and not letting her intense curiosity take over. "Principal Montenegro is going to need the whole story, especially how you figured out the culprit. That's the only way we can prove we're innocent. And if you're going to tell her when she comes, you might as well let us in on the story now."

Nora sighed, her face getting even redder. "Okay, you're right but here's the thing," she said, giving them each a fierce glare. "This is information you take to your grave. You have to swear, on your honor, that you will never reveal it to a single soul, ever."

Maddie was now desperate to learn what this secret was!

"Promise," the three of them said, nearly in unison. Clearly the boys were as eager as Maddie to find out what was so classified.

"And swear on your honor," Nora said seriously.

"I swear on my honor to never, ever breathe a word of this ever," Maddie said, leaning forward.

"Me too," Jack said. He had started another sketch, but now the pencil was still in his hand as he stared at Nora.

"I double-swear," Henry agreed, his seat still as he looked expectantly at Nora.

Nora let out a loud breath, shook her head, closed her eyes, and then spoke. "I," she said, "am Astrid."

"Wait, *what*?" Henry asked, incredulous.

"Honest Astrid's Advice on Everything," Nora said, defeated. "I'm the one who writes it. No one knows, not even Ms. Holt. I submitted it anonymously one day as a joke when I was upset no one reads serious journalism, and then it just kind of took off."

Maddie's brain was exploding. Nora—serious, adult-in-a-seventh-grader's-body *Nora*—was effervescent, wisecracking, and super-insightful Astrid? It was impossible.

"No way!" Henry said, his eyes wide.

"Wow," Jack added. His pencil had slipped out of his hand, but he didn't seem to notice. "Just—wow."

"I know, it's so embarrassing," Nora whimpered, her eyes downcast. "I keep promising myself I'll stop because it's such a silly column and it keeps people from reading anything meaningful, but—"

"But it's the reason everyone reads the paper," Jack finished.

"Yeah," Nora said quietly. "If I want to keep building my clipping file of articles for my college and internship applications, I need the paper to have strong circulation numbers. So I can't stop."

"Of course you can't stop!" Maddie exclaimed. What was Nora talking about? For someone so smart, she was being shockingly obtuse. (Maddie also couldn't imagine a seventh grader thinking about college already—but clearly that was Nora.) "That column is the best thing in the paper!" She knew this was the wrong thing to say the moment it came out of her mouth, even before Nora slumped down in her seat.

"Okay, guys, this is interesting and all," Jack said,

glancing at the clock. "But talking about Astrid can wait. Nora, you telling us who broke into Sasha's locker can't."

Maddie bit her lip—it was true. She'd just have to make things okay with Nora later.

"Yeah," Nora said, straightening up, a frown on her face. "But you're not going to believe it. I don't believe it."

"Just tell us!" Henry practically shouted.

"It was Louis Nichols," Nora said.

Louis? Nora was right—Maddie didn't believe it. Louis was one of the sweetest, smartest kids in the grade. He was nice to everyone and everyone liked him, even Sasha! Maddie had heard her call him "a teddy bear boy" a few weeks ago at dance team practice. Louis would never do something like break into someone's locker and steal something.

"That doesn't make sense," Jack said, his brows scrunched.

"I know," Nora agreed, sitting up straight. She was back to her crisp, cool self. "But first of all, the handwriting on this paper with the locker combinations is definitely Louis's—he has a way of making block letters that curl on the *a*'s and *s*'s—he did it on an Astrid letter he sent me. Second, in the letter he mentioned something about research—his skills are strong. He'd totally find that tape trick to keep an exit door open. And like we guessed, he's an office volunteer so it would be easy for him to find out the schedule of administrators and janitors passing by the A alcove every day. All he'd have to do is look."

Nora's ability to gather and process information was truly impressive. Though the clues they'd all found had helped.

"And if he works in the office, that's probably how Louis got Sasha's locker combination too," Henry said slowly, rubbing his chin. "But I still—"

"Nice work, folks."

Maddie nearly fell out of her seat at the interruption of Principal Montenegro's voice cutting through the room as she walked in through the open door. Clearly she'd been standing outside and had heard everything.

"Nora, that's some good investigative digging on your part," the principal said, smiling at all of them for the first time. "I apologize for keeping you all here, but I'm grateful for the teamwork and school spirit you showed, working together. You are free to go." She was still smiling as she handed each of them a late pass to second period.

Henry was grinning and Jack reached over to give Maddie a high five. She slapped his hand with vigor, relief fizzing up inside her like soda bubbles.

But as she stood up and slung her bag over one shoulder, the bubbles fizzled out, leaving an emptiness behind. Which was weird—this *was* a relief. Obviously. She *should* feel like a shaken-up soda. So why were the bubbles gone? Across the table, Nora looked serious—though she probably always looked serious—as she hoisted on her odd leather bag. Maddie still couldn't believe Nora was Astrid.

"So, we're just supposed to go to class now?" Jack asked, hovering at the door. He didn't look as excited as he had before either.

"Correct," Principal Montenegro said warmly. "Again, I'm sorry for the inconvenience—we went on the information we had."

That wasn't much of an apology, not that Maddie really expected one. The principal was probably worried about being sued or something.

Jack opened the door and headed out, Henry right behind him and Nora on his heels. Maddie rushed to leave next, not wanting to be stuck in the awkward position of making small talk with the principal. But Principal Montenegro was studying the paper with the locker combinations and had pulled out her cell phone.

"So that's that," Jack said quietly, once all four of them were in the hall.

"Yeah," Maddie said, unsure of why everything felt so wrong when she should just be happy she was finally out of that room. But it did. Still, as Jack had said, that was that. The only thing to do now was head to class. "Okay, well, see you guys later, I guess."

She turned and headed down the hall, shaking her head to clear out the doubts and move past what had simply been a very strange morning.

CHAPTER 8

NORA

Something was not right. Nora couldn't put her finger on it. She was certain Louis was the culprit: She was positive about his handwriting, and every piece of evidence fit. And yet—something was off. Or missing. Something big. Nora's instincts for a story were always on point, and she was positive they'd only scratched the surface of this story.

"Wait," Nora called to Maddie, Jack, and Henry, who had all begun walking away. As they turned, she looked closely at each of them: The crinkle between Maddie's brows, the way Jack's lips were pressed together, the way Henry had not made one stupid remark about them being free—they felt it too.

"Are we positive Louis did this?" Nora asked.

Henry ran a hand through his hair and then tugged at it. "I get that all the stuff we found adds up, and everything you said is obviously true . . ."

"But it doesn't make sense," Nora finished.

"It really doesn't," Maddie agreed in a rush, clearly relieved to hear their words.

"Louis is the guy who sticks up for kids that get picked on and tells new sixth graders where their classrooms are, even if it makes him late to class," Jack said. "He's not someone who breaks into lockers and steals stuff."

"There's more to this story," Nora said, now more certain than ever. "And we need to get to the bottom of it."

Maddie and Henry were nodding.

"Let's meet at snack," Nora said, straightening her satchel and turning toward her honors class down the hall. Snack was right after second period and would give them a chance to figure this out. "We'll start investigating then."

Nora spent the remainder of her English class fretting. Well, after she answered two of Ms. Boon's discussion questions on *The Good Earth*, which was her favorite book of the year so far, she fretted.

The worries kept piling up.

First, there was definitely more to the story. Why would kind and friendly Louis have broken into

Sasha's locker? They'd been the ones to get him in trouble with the principal, so it was up to them to figure out what was really going on.

Then there was the problem of the backpack. Sasha held the four of them responsible, and until it was in her hands, they were all vulnerable. Sasha was disturbingly good at digging up information—confidential information. Before today, only Nora's parents and older brother, Khai, knew that Nora was Astrid. And initially Nora had been sure Sasha was bluffing that she had dirt on Nora—but then she'd remembered an odd incident a few months ago. Nora had been shopping with Mom when suddenly she'd turned and seen Sasha surprisingly close. She'd been reaching for a box of cereal, and at the time Nora assumed that was all she was doing. But now Nora realized there was more to it: Sasha had been eavesdropping because Nora had been complaining to Mom about Astrid. It was actually possible Sasha hadn't even wanted the cereal and that she'd come close solely to listen in on Nora's conversation. So yes, there was no doubt that Sasha knew something that could hurt Nora if it ever got out.

Nora groaned and dropped her head onto her book, because thanks to Sasha, she'd had to tell the others

Astrid's true identity. Even if they were able to keep Sasha from spilling their secrets, could she really trust Jack, Maddie, and especially Henry to keep their promises never to tell? People speculated about Astrid's true identity all the time—it would be so easy to let it slip out, especially for Henry, who seemed to have real issues keeping his mouth shut at crucial times. And having them know something so embarrassing made Nora feel like her skin had peeled away, leaving her raw and exposed.

Nora tried to focus her thoughts. Worrying about Astrid wouldn't help anything. What she could do, however, was to help figure out what was going on with Louis. And make sure Sasha got that pack back. The bell rang for snack, and Nora was out of her seat so fast it nearly toppled over behind her.

"Finish the book tonight," Ms. Boon called over the din of people pushing out chairs and talking. "And enjoy the rest of your day."

That was a tall order for Nora. She hustled out of the room and into the hall, which was quickly filling with students. Being short made navigating crowds challenging (even many of the sixth graders were taller than Nora, which was just insulting), but Nora had perfected the art of leading with her elbows. As a result, she was one of the first students to reach the cafeteria for the twenty-minute snack break. Which posed a dilemma: Where to sit? Nora never came to snack—she spent this time in the newspaper office. Lunch too. But given the locked social hierarchy of middle school (the high schoolers were upstairs and had their own cafeteria), she knew it would be a mistake to sit at the wrong table.

"Nora, that was a great interview with the town council on the bill to put a new stop sign on Garden Avenue," Erlan, an eighth grader on the paper, said as he passed. He was a political reporter for the *Sentinel*, writing about government stuff on the state and national levels. Nora had a feeling only high schoolers and parents read his articles—they were real journalism and often long—but he had hits on everything he published and a following of people who got into discussions in the comments.

No one ever started conversations in Nora's comments. But it was nice that a few people—very few—like Erlan read her articles and enjoyed them.

"Thanks," Nora said.

Erlan headed over to a table with some of the other

kids who were into gaming, leaving Nora standing alone and starting to feel a bit self-conscious.

"Hey," Maddie said, coming up beside her. Maddie had shed her pink messenger bag and unzipped her hoodie to reveal a shirt with flamingos prancing across it. It was unique: the kind of thing worn by someone who knew she looked good in anything. Which was definitely true of graceful, athletic Maddie. Nora felt a bit like a garden gnome next to her.

"Maddie!" Michelle B. called, waving from a table that was obviously prime real estate next to the window. She was sitting with a few other members of the dance team, as well as some girls and guys who played soccer. In other words, a popular-kids table. "Are you ditching us?"

Maddie laughed, waving back. "Yup," she called back. "Nora and I have business."

"Get her to tell you who Astrid is," Michelle B. demanded, but she was smiling. Michelle B. was like Maddie: popular but nice to everyone. Kind of the exact opposite of Sasha, who was holding court at what was clearly the best table in the huge room, next to the window and in the corner. It was filled with the popular elite from sixth, seventh, and eighth grades. In other words, people who looked down on everyone else.

Michelle B.'s words were small stones in Nora's belly as she followed Maddie to a table on the far side of the room, in a less populated section of the cafeteria. How long would it take before Maddie or one of the others decided Nora's Astrid identity was too juicy not to share?

"So listen," Maddie said, sitting down on the bench across from Nora and pulling a packet of sunflower seeds out of her pocket. "I want to say more about the whole"—she lowered her voice—"Astrid thing."

The small stones were growing larger. Nora, who had an apple but no room in her stomach now that it was full of rocks, nodded stiffly as Jack arrived and settled next to Nora, a Ziploc bag of cheesy crackers in one hand.

Obviously he had heard Maddie's remark because he looked at Nora, his brows knit. "Nora, that column is incredible."

"I read it," Henry added, coming up so quietly Nora didn't see him until he was on her other side. He had obviously gone through the line for the free school snack and was already ripping open the bag of no-brand potato chips.

"It's fluff," Nora said dismissively. "The kind of thing that belongs on social media, not in a real newspaper."

"It's not though," Maddie said. She had opened the pouch of seeds but stopped to look directly at Nora. "You really helped me with your suggestions about what to say when people act like there's something wrong with how my mom lives her life."

"How does your mom live her life?" Henry asked immediately. And not surprisingly—Henry was predictable in his zest to know everything.

Maddie arched a brow at Nora, who stifled a giggle. Which was very unlike her—Nora was not a giggler. But Henry was being just so, well, *Henry*.

"My mom is a lawyer, and after my parents split up when I was little, she got this great job offer in Boston," Maddie said. "She and my dad decided it would be better for me to stay here with him, because he's a homebody and she'd be working crazy hours, so he'd be the best caretaker of a little kid."

"Makes sense," Henry said, stuffing chips in his mouth and speaking over them. "What's the problem?"

Although Henry's manners were disgusting, Nora appreciated that he didn't jump to the conclusion most people jumped to—the one that had bothered Maddie so much she'd written a letter to Astrid.

"Some people think it's the job of the woman to take care of the kid, end of story. Like, no one says a dad isn't a good dad because he works or shares custody. But people sometimes act like my mom isn't a good mom because she has a job she works hard at and doesn't see me every night. I hate that, so I asked Astrid—um, Nora—what to do about it." Maddie grinned at the memory of the column, and Nora felt a strange swell of something sweet and warm in her chest. "She said she was sorry that I'd encountered people stuck in the last century and that I should send them to her if they need any information about how to use the internet."

Henry and Jack snickered appreciatively, and the warm, sweet feeling spread through her whole body like a cup of homemade hot chocolate.

"And also to let them know that my mom's job paid for my new phone and our ladies' trip to Maui, where we stayed in a three-star hotel on the beach and went snorkeling with sea turtles, so I'm pretty happy with how she parents me," Maddie finished.

"For real?" Jack asked. He'd been shoveling in cheesy crackers but paused, looking jealous. "You guys went to Hawaii? I would love to go there—painting those flowers and that ocean—the colors are beyond incredible."

Maddie grinned. "Yeah, my mom is super good at her job, so she gets raises all the time."

Henry mumbled something that sounded like "must be nice."

"What?" Nora asked, turning to him.

Henry stuffed in more chips. "That's a great Astrid answer." He gave Nora a thumbs-up, his fingers shiny with grease.

"Yeah, seriously, Nora," Jack said. "It was perfect."

The sweet, warm feeling: It was pride. Nora was feeling proud of a column she'd written for Astrid. Which was ridiculous: Astrid was fluff.

And yet—it had helped Maddie with a problem that was real. Nora's advice had made a difference.

"So what's the plan to free Louis and get Sasha off our backs?" Henry asked, scrunching up his chips bag and moving on to the small orange that was part of his snack tray.

This time Nora was the one grinning at Maddie.

"Um, I'm not sure we're freeing Louis," Maddie said, grinning back at Nora.

"Sure we are," Henry said as he ripped open the orange, spraying Nora with tiny juice droplets. "We're freeing him from whatever pushed him to commit theft and cross Sasha, which is even more dangerous."

That was actually a good point.

"Whatever," Jack said, brushing crumbs off his hands. "The bottom line is we need a strategy."

A group of kids from the after-school art club walked by, and Jack waved as they greeted him.

"Do we have any idea why Louis would need that backpack so badly he'd break into her locker to get it?" Maddie asked after they'd passed. She pulled some seeds out of the bag and crunched down on them.

"Maybe she's plotting a bank robbery and the plans are in the backpack," Henry said. Orange juice was dribbling down his chin, and he swiped at it with a napkin.

Jack's mouth puckered up in distaste as he watched. "That seems unlikely," he said.

But Henry's words had Nora suddenly backtracking. *"Plans in the backpack,"* she repeated.

Henry's brows scrunched. "I was kidding."

"I know, I just—we've been thinking Sasha wanted her backpack returned because it's designer, but what if what she really wants—and what Louis needed—was something *inside* her pack?" Nora said, pieces clicking together. Jack was nodding. "She told me she wanted her stuff back," he said. "And really this makes more sense. What would Louis want with her backpack?"

Henry pressed his fingertips together, looking pleased. "Yes, this is progress," he said. "The item in question is something *inside* that bag."

"But we still don't know why Louis would want anything from Sasha," Jack pointed out.

Nora sagged a bit. He was right. They were no closer to figuring anything out. Anything that mattered anyway.

"What connects Sasha and Louis?" Henry asked. "I've never seen them hang out."

"They don't exactly have the same friends," Jack said.

"I don't really know either of them well," Maddie said, nodding as some seventh graders passed. "I mean, Sasha's in dance and so I know how great she thinks she is. But I don't think she has anything against

Louis because a few weeks ago she called him a teddy bear boy, and that's a Sasha compliment."

"What does she call me?" Henry asked, then held up a hand. "Forget it, I don't want to know."

Nora could tell from Maddie's expression Henry was right—he did not want to know. No one could be mean like Sasha.

"I don't hang out with Louis or anything, but I've had classes with him so I know he's a good guy." Jack said. "I definitely don't know what he'd need from Sasha. But I do know he'd never do something like this without a really good reason."

They all nodded. There was no way Louis would do this unless he was desperate.

Henry had stuffed his orange peels into his chips bag. "It sounds like our next step is to talk to the people who do know each of them. That way we can find out what connects them and hopefully figure out what's in that backpack."

"I'm also wondering if we should tell Principal Montenegro we think Louis had a good reason for what he did," Maddie suggested.

"Why would she care what we think?" Henry asked.

Maddie shrugged. "She might not, but it seems worth a shot."

"And if we go by the office, we can see if there's any new intel," Nora said.

"That's true," Maddie said. "Let's go."

They dropped their trash in bins and then headed out into the hall.

"So who should we talk to about Sasha and Louis?" Jack asked, readjusting his bag over his shoulder.

"His sister Emma's on the dance team," Maddie said as they walked down the hall. There were posters for the Starlight Gala everywhere, along with flyers for clubs and reminders to recycle. "I don't really know her but I'm sure she'd want to help free her brother."

Emma was the only sixth grader to have made the dance team, and she was so good she'd even made the Gala squad. Nora had seen her and Louis chatting in the halls more than once—which meant they were probably close enough that Emma would know something. Talking to Emma was a great idea.

"I can also ask other people on the team," Maddie added, almost bumping into a group of sixth graders huddled around a phone. "Some of them know Sasha a lot better than I do."

"That's a good start," Henry said.

He was interrupted by Mr. Jenkins hurrying down the hall and shouting, "That better not be a phone out!"

The sixth graders scattered.

"I can talk to Javier and Dash," Jack said. "I know them from art club, and they hang out with Louis a lot."

That was another good idea.

"Shiloh and Charlie hang out with them too, and Jack and I know them from the paper," Nora said, glad to have something to add. "I'll ask them."

Jack looked at Henry. "So who do you know from after-school stuff?"

Henry was still for a moment. "I do stuff at home after school," he said.

"What, come up with stupid jokes?" Jack asked.

Henry gave him a cold look. "I take care of my brother and sister," he said shortly.

They'd reached the office, which was a good thing because the tension between Jack and Henry was annoying Nora. Jack had been a jerk on purpose, and Henry not joking in response had to mean he was seriously bothered by Jack. Not what they needed on their investigative team.

Nora led the way into the office and saw Principal

Montenegro, her back to them, talking on the phone.

"I understand your concern," she was saying. "But your son is refusing to cooperate. He admits to the locker break-in and theft but won't give back the item he stole or tell us why he took it."

Nora froze. Louis was *refusing* to return the pack?

"Yes, right now this offense is grounds for expulsion," Principal Montenegro continued. "But perhaps Louis will share more when you and your wife arrive. I'll see you both at two thirty sharp."

Nora backed out of the office, her thoughts racing. Louis was willing to risk expulsion rather than return the backpack?

The others were hurrying down the hall and Nora hustled after them.

"Listen," Maddie began when they had rounded the corner, but then they heard footsteps coming down the hall. A moment later, Sasha, tall and golden, her shimmery brown hair a cascading wave behind her, appeared. When she saw them, she stumbled slightly.

"What's going on?" she asked sharply.

"Principal Montenegro released us, since none of us took your stupid backpack," Jack said, with venom that made Nora flinch.

"So then who did?" Sasha demanded, walking up to them. She smelled like coconut and vanilla, and the scent gave Nora an instant headache. Or maybe it was Sasha herself who was making Nora's temples throb.

"Like we'd tell you," Henry scoffed. His usually affable expression was replaced with hard features and a slight sneer.

Nora's whole body clenched up. That had not been a good thing to say.

"So you guys know but won't tell me," Sasha said, eyes narrowing slightly.

Nora saw Henry's shoulders sag as he realized his mistake.

"It's not our problem anymore," Jack said, but the venom was gone and he sounded hesitant.

Sasha noticed his weakness and smiled a tight, chilly smile. "It is, actually," she said. "I will hold all of you accountable until my possessions are back in my hands."

"We can't control when you get your bag back," Maddie said in a pleading tone.

"And that," Sasha said triumphantly, "is not my problem."

Clearly pleased with how things had gone, she

spun delicately on one heel and sashayed back around the corner.

"I should have kept my mouth shut," Henry said bitterly.

"That's an understatement," Jack muttered.

Henry blinked in surprise, then shrugged like he couldn't care less. Though Nora saw the flash of hurt in his eyes and she didn't blame him, Jack made no secret of how little he cared for Henry. Which was kind of surprising: Jack was a pretty nice guy, and while Henry was silly, he'd come through today.

The bell ending snack break rang and Nora nearly leapt out of her skin.

"Okay, the clock is ticking," Henry said, his voice taut as the halls began to fill. "We have until the end of the day to save Louis."

"And," Nora added miserably, "to save ourselves."

CHAPTER 9

JACK

Jack's jaw was clenched as he headed to class, Henry next to him. The bell had rung, ending snack, and it turned out the girls were going in the opposite direction. Which meant Jack, who was still feeling sick from the Sasha encounter, was stuck with Henry.

"This is bad," Henry said quietly as they passed the science lab. Jack squeezed his fist—obviously it was bad! Why did Henry have to spell it out?

"Hi, Jack," Ainyr, a girl from art club, called as he passed.

Jack nodded and smiled, but then huffed as Henry walked too close and bumped into him.

"Watch it," Jack said shortly. Yes, it was crowded in the hall but everyone else was able to navigate without hitting into something or someone.

"Listen, I don't know what your problem with me is but—" Henry started, and Jack turned, both fists now clenched.

"Really, you don't know what my problem is?" Jack said, the words bubbling up like lava. "You don't remember basically accusing me of being the one to . . ." He lowered his voice, though it was hard. ". . . break into Sasha's locker?"

It was a relief to speak what had been corrosive inside him for the past few hours. Jack was laid-back about many things, but being falsely accused was most definitely not one of them. He wasn't sure why Henry had chosen to slander him—racism, Jack being into art and not sports, or whatever—but he was quite sure he wasn't okay with it. And it was time for Henry to know that.

Henry nodded. "Yeah, I remember. I was there."

Was Henry deliberately being an idiot to infuriate Jack even more?

"And you don't think I have a problem with that?" Jack asked sarcastically.

Henry looked confused. "Out of everyone you had the most reason to not like her—that racist stuff she said to you was really messed up. I might've broken into her locker if she said that to me."

Jack's fists slowly unclenched. It had not occurred to him that Henry was bothered by the story Jack had told, that he had thought more about it. And Henry was right—Nora being upset that Sasha knew she was Astrid was bad, but not as bad as what Sasha had said to Jack. Jack hadn't taken the time to think of that—but Henry had. He had heard what Jack said and gotten upset on Jack's behalf. And imagined that in Jack's shoes he might be angry enough to lash out at Sasha.

While Jack had never bothered to put himself in Henry's shoes. Or wonder why Henry was so worried about Sasha.

"It just seemed like you had a really legit reason to want revenge or whatever," Henry went on. "Like the Avengers going after Thanos. Or when—"

"I get it," Jack interrupted, nodding. "And yeah, what she said bugged me. A lot."

Henry shrugged. "So, that's all I was thinking—I wasn't trying to accuse you. I mean, I guess I kind of did, actually, but I didn't mean it like I thought you were lying or something."

"I get it," Jack said. Because he finally did get it. "Thanks."

"So you're not going to try to vaporize me or anything anymore?" Henry asked, grinning.

Jack shook his head and snickered. "No, we're good."

"Cool, because we need to save that for Sasha," Henry said.

It was a fair point.

They were passing the hallway that was blocked off for the Starlight Gala and Jack could see one of his paintings, this one of his neighbor's flower garden. Seeing it, he got a sick feeling all over again: Why had Ms. Antonov chosen that one? It was bad enough his dad and brother would see his art, but she had to select a picture of vibrant pink roses and lavender-hued hydrangeas?

"I don't get how your family isn't super excited about this," Henry said, gesturing toward the display. "Do they know how good you are?"

Jack shrugged awkwardly because it was possible he hadn't fully explained about his family. Yes, they wanted him to play baseball and, yes, they didn't get why he spent time on non-baseball things. And yes, they hassled him about it—a lot. But it was also true that Jack might not have told them how much he loved art. Or showed them much of what he'd made. Why bother? They'd think it was stupid. They'd think it was wimpy. They'd think *Jack* was wimpy. And maybe he was. So Jack just wanted his art and his family to stay separate.

"If I had a skill like this, I'd use it to make counterfeit money or something," Henry said in his goofy way.

Jack rolled his eyes. "I can see you make your family proud," he joked, happy he actually wanted to joke with Henry.

But instead of joking back, Henry drooped and his eyes grew distant.

"Yeah," he said quietly. "I give them so much to be proud of."

With that he headed down the hall, leaving Jack in front of his English classroom wondering what exactly Henry meant.

Jack arrived at his fourth-period history class too late to talk to anyone (he always had to sprint across the building from his English class third period), but Mr. Patel was assigning a group project so when it came time to select partners, Jack headed straight over to Javier and Dash, Louis's friends.

"Want to work together?" he asked, though he was pretty sure he knew the answer. Jack's drawing skills made him an excellent group member for most projects. And he couldn't lie—that felt good.

"Yeah, awesome," Dash said enthusiastically.

Amirah, a girl from the basketball team, came up to them. "Would you guys want to do something on the history of girls in sports?" she asked, pulling up her chair and sitting. Amirah was smart and funny and not one of the lazy people who made everyone else in the group do everything, so Jack was glad she'd joined them. "Those guys are too archaic to appreciate what a good idea it is." She gestured to Rudy, Eric, and Steve, who were on the boys' team.

"Gemma could take all three of you," Amirah called to them. Gemma was in eighth grade and the star of the girls' team. Even Dad and Matt talked about Gemma's skills after games—and it was middle school.

Eric and Steve scoffed, but Rudy grinned ruefully. "That's the truth," he said. Then he headed for the door—he only stayed for part of history class. Jack wasn't sure why, but he had never been interested enough to ask. Especially today, when he had way more important questions.

"Hey, have Louis and Sasha been hanging out lately?" Jack asked. He pulled out his pencils to start sketching, to help with his thinking. And to help with their project of course.

Dash's forehead scrunched, and Javier looked from Dash to Jack. "Why?" he asked. "Does it have something to do with why Louis got called out of second period and hasn't been back since?"

"It might," Jack said, deciding he wasn't going to reveal everything to them—he had no idea what Louis might prefer to keep secret.

"I knew it was only a matter of time before Sasha started stashing bodies in her backyard," Amirah said wryly.

The three boys laughed.

"We laugh but she is almost that mean," Amirah said.

She wasn't wrong.

"Okay, folks, I'm passing out your graphic organizers," Mr. Patel said, making his way around the room. "Choose your roles and then get to it."

"I'm recorder," Amirah announced as Mr. Patel handed them their paper.

"And an excellent leader," Mr. Patel said with a

smile. He was the nicest teacher in school, and unlike most of the other teachers, his classes were never boring.

"Jack, you're the artist, obviously, so that leaves research to you guys," Amirah said to Dash and Javier as she pulled out a pen. "But first we're answering Jack's question."

Amirah was the best.

"Sometimes they talk," Dash said. "Like in class or whatever. Louis doesn't hang out with her or her friends, but they don't have a problem with him." He shrugged. "At least not that he's told me."

"Me neither," Javier said. He was now on the school laptop Mr. Patel had given them for research.

"Reliable sources only," Amirah reminded him.

"I know," Javier said. Between Mr. Patel and Ms. MacCullough, the whole school knew you only ever did research from reliable sources that were based on facts. That was what Jack needed here—he could speculate all day about what might have gone on between Sasha and Louis, but what he needed were facts.

"Has Louis been acting strange at all lately?" Jack pressed, shading in the rim of a basketball hoop. He wasn't sure what sports they'd focus on for the project but basketball was a good bet, given Amirah's status on the team.

Dash shrugged and Javier was now distracted by an article he'd found on the school's encyclopedia website. They were no help.

"I saw Louis talking to Rudy a week or two ago—like a real conversation, serious and stuff," Amirah said, looking up from the organizer, where she was writing down their names. "That's strange, right? Louis is nice but he stays in his lane."

Both Javier and Dash had stopped what they were doing, so clearly they agreed.

"Really?" Dash asked, looking surprised. "What would he have to talk to Rudy about?"

"That's why I thought it was strange," Amirah pointed out. "Unless Louis has sudden aspirations to be a jock, I can't think of anything."

Jack was nodding. This did seem strange.

"You know," Dash said, sounding thoughtful, "for the past few days I haven't seen Louis much."

"Me neither," Javier agreed. "Plus he missed out on gaming last night, and that was strange too."

Jack was smiling; these weren't just facts, they were clues. Clues that led them to their next person of interest: Rudy.

And with the clock ticking, that was exactly what they needed.

CHAPTER 10

HENRY

Henry was busy piling up his tray with food when Nora came up behind him. "Grab me some fries, okay?" she asked. "I'll be at the table."

"Sure," Henry said agreeably, picking up an extra plate of fries. Lunch was his favorite meal of the day because you could eat as much as you wanted and not have to pay anything.

Three months ago, exactly four weeks after Henry had ruined everything for his family, he'd overheard Mom and Dad talking about ways they could cut back expenses. Dad had asked about the pricey grocery bill, and Mom had said it was due to "Henry eating us out of house and home." That was when Henry started going to the library before school each day to get a breakfast of the free granola bars Ms. MacCullough put out, eating school snacks whether he liked them or not, and scarfing down so much lunch he barely had room for an after-school snack (except for peanut butter, but that wasn't expensive) and dinner. It was the least he could do considering it was his fault they didn't have enough money in the first place. Henry scanned his card at the register, then picked up his tray and headed for the table where Jack, Maddie, and Nora were waiting. Henry and his friends Francis, Judy, Lena, and Nathan usually sat along the non-window wall. They'd known one another since elementary school, and it was both fun and comfortable to be with them. It would be a little weird sitting with new people—and it would definitely not be fun or comfortable. Though at least Jack didn't hate him anymore.

Henry wove between tables and almost stopped when he heard two sixth graders debating the best kind of chips. They were both wrong—neither had said barbecue—but Henry would have to educate them later, after either they'd returned the bag and whatever was inside to Sasha or Henry's life had completely imploded.

He was almost at the table when Sasha intercepted him. "Serving food to everyone?" she asked, towering over him. Henry saw Jack, Maddie, and Nora fall silent as they turned to stare at the exchange. "Just like your dad."

Henry almost dropped the tray.

"Careful there," Sasha said, smiling an arctic smile.

Henry walked the last few steps to the table on quivering legs and deposited the tray, his hands shaking so much Nora reached out to steady it so the food didn't slide off.

"Glad to see you're working together to find my backpack," Sasha said to them all. "I expect it in my hands by the end of the day. Oh, and be sure not to open it—if it's been opened, our deal is off."

She strode back to her table while Henry pressed his palms together, realizing they were slick with sweat. He glanced around and was relieved to see no one else had been close enough to hear what Sasha had said to him about his dad.

"She is evil," Maddie said, shaking her head as she reached over and patted Henry's shoulder, which was surprisingly comforting. "I don't know what she meant about your dad and you don't have to tell us, but she has something bad on me too. We're finding that backpack to make sure it never gets out."

"Thanks," Henry said. He wasn't sure that was possible, but it felt good to hear her say it with such conviction.

"Even if I do decide to tell people about Astrid, which I won't, but if I did, I'd want to do it on my terms, not hers," Nora said, her eyes hard as she looked at Sasha, now ensconced at the golden table.

"She wants to do that to my brother too," Jack said, biting off each word, "tell something about him that is his business and his choice when and if he shares it."

Maddie's eyes widened. "Is your brother gay?" she whispered. "And he doesn't want your dad to know, like you and your art?"

Jack smiled. "No, my dad would be fine with that—he's really supportive of kids on his team who come out and stuff. It's something else." He was no longer smiling. "Something that only my dad and I know—I can't figure out how Sasha found out."

Maddie's face puckered like she'd eaten a bad banana. "I can tell you how she found mine—she was there. And she made a video."

Henry was so intrigued by this he almost forgot Sasha's threats against him.

"That day Coach Faizal made a mistake and called me out as last in drills—I kind of went off in the locker room," Maddie said, looping her ponytail through her fingers. "I said some nasty stuff about the coach—nothing I meant, you know, just the dumb stuff you say when you're angry and the person can't hear you. Well, they can't hear you unless someone decides to take a secret video."

Henry was disgusted but not surprised by the story.

"Why would she do that?" Nora asked, poking her fork into a thermos of spaghetti she'd brought from home. "Who makes a video in the locker room filming their own teammate?"

"Someone diabolical," Jack said. He had ripped open his cafeteria sandwich and bit into it roughly.

Which reminded Henry to eat. He didn't exactly feel like it, not with his stomach frothing like the inside of a washing machine, but he needed to fill up. He picked up a fry and chewed, the salt and grease coating his tongue. He wiped his hands on his jeans, then passed the extra plate of fries and ketchup to Nora, who smiled her thanks.

"You know, she found out about Astrid when she overheard me talking to my mom about it when we were shopping at Canon Market," Nora said, opening a packet of ketchup. "It never occurred to me until today to wonder why she was so close to us that she heard what I was saying."

"She was probably there shopping with her family," Jack said, his sandwich paused halfway to his mouth. "And when she saw you, she followed you to eavesdrop."

Nora nodded decisively. "This must be what Sasha does," she declared. "She gathers dirt on people, the stuff they don't want public, and saves it until she needs it to blackmail them into doing something for her."

Henry nodded. This was certainly what she was doing to him—to all of them. He stuffed the last of his fries in his mouth and picked up his first burger.

"So this is what's happening with Louis," Maddie said. She had finished the strange-looking chips and dip she'd brought from home (the dip was an odd greenish beige, though Maddie had clearly enjoyed it despite its mold-like appearance) and was now crunching into an apple. "She found out something Louis wanted to keep private and threatened to reveal it unless he did what she said. And either what she wants him to do or what she found out is so bad that he stole her bag to stop her."

"Which means we need to figure out what the dirt is and why it's so terrible that Louis's risking expulsion to keep it hidden," Nora said, sliding a few fries through ketchup.

"I agree we should find out about Sasha blackmailing Louis and free him," Maddie said. "But shouldn't we try to find the backpack and save ourselves first?"

"I think it's the same thing," Nora said slowly. "Louis is hiding whatever's in the backpack and Sasha needs it back. The key to helping him and stopping her from threatening all of us is figuring out what they're both after."

Henry considered this. If their theory was correct and Sasha was blackmailing Louis, then the only way to free him was to get her to stop. The only way to make her stop was to find out what he was hiding in the first place and how Sasha was using it against him. And when they knew that, they'd know what was in the backpack—and that would be the key to getting it back. So yes, helping Louis helped them. Unless of course Sasha really did just want the bag itself back— but that seemed less likely now, given her insistence they not open it and Louis's refusal to return it.

"So what did you guys find out?" he asked, digging back into his burger.

A group of girls from their class walked by, a few

calling out to Maddie, who waved. Once they'd passed, Maddie leaned forward. "Okay, Emma's absent today, so I couldn't ask her what she knows about her brother's relationship with Sasha," she said, "but I did find out that Sasha has bullied some of the other girls on the dance team. Lena told me that Sasha made fun of Pilar's accent, but Pilar shut her down, saying Sasha could talk when she was fluent in two languages, and until then she could keep her mouth shut."

Henry was not surprised—Pilar was not someone to mess with.

"Pilar handled that well," Jack said admiringly. He took his last bite of sandwich and balled up the cellophane wrapper.

Henry had finished his fries and first burger and was now halfway through the second. It turned out he could eat even when his belly was on spin mode.

"I talked to Dash, Javier, and Amirah," Jack said. "And they said two pretty interesting things: first, that Louis has been acting kind of weird the past two days, and second, that they saw him talking to Rudy, which is—"

"Totally off!" Nora crowed. "I heard the exact same thing from Shiloh and a couple of other people in the newspaper office. They all passed Louis talking with Rudy in the hall and thought it was super strange."

"They have zero in common," Jack said, his brow creasing as he considered this. "What could they have been talking about?"

"Maybe Rudy saw Louis do something and Louis wanted him to keep it secret?" Maddie suggested. "Like trying out for basketball and making a fool of himself?"

"I don't think Louis would try out for basketball," Nora said.

"But before today we wouldn't have thought he'd break into someone's locker," Henry pointed out. "I don't know, though, looking dumb at a tryout doesn't seem like that big a deal."

"Maybe Rudy asked Louis to help him cheat on a test," Jack said. "Rudy's not a great student and Louis totally is. Maybe Rudy somehow guilted Louis into it and he doesn't want to get caught."

"And maybe Sasha was there, eavesdropping like she did on Nora in the grocery store," Henry said, his detective skills once again paying off. It was possible he had a future in this.

"I'm not sure if cheating is the secret, but I think

you're right about Sasha overhearing something," Nora said, standing up and sliding her reusable lunch containers back in her leather bag-thing. "So let's go find Rudy and ask him."

As the others stood and gathered their belongings, Henry stuffed the last of his burger in his mouth and his three packets of chocolate chip cookies in his hoodie pocket for later.

They had exactly two hours and eight minutes to find that backpack before Sasha spilled their secrets, and they couldn't afford to waste a second of it.

CHAPTER 11

NORA

"Astrid was the one who told me to talk to him!" an eighth-grade girl walking by gushed as the four made their way to the tray counter so Henry and Jack could bus their trays.

"She's amazing!" the girl's friend raved. Nora cringed, hoping Maddie, Jack, and especially Henry would act natural and not blow her cover.

Maddie glanced back casually and raised a brow at Nora, but the boys plowed ahead to dump their trash and trays, allowing Nora to breathe a sigh of relief.

The two eighth graders ignored Nora as she passed, and for one fleeting second, Nora wondered what they'd think knowing that "amazing" advice had come from the seventh grader going by. She also wondered which letter it was, which guy had been talked to, and to what result. Sometimes Astrid gave advice to girls needing encouragement to ask someone out, but other times she advised girls who had been talked down to or treated as unimportant. These letters—telling girls how to make their voices heard—were some of Nora's favorites to write.

At the trash cans, she dumped her ketchup wrappers, then put her fries plate in the rubber bin by the dish-washing window. She did a final napkin wipe of her fingers—cafeteria fries were greasy but so good—then followed the others out into the hall. Rudy, like the other basketball players, would be in the gym.

The hall was nearly empty, and quiet after the crowd noise of the cafeteria. It was a relief to leave that and the soggy burger smell behind.

"So, did you hear that?" Maddie asked, walking so close to Nora that their arms bumped. "About how amazing Astrid is?"

Nora attempted to shrug this off but she could not stop the warm feeling—the pride—from washing over her. Was writing Astrid making her shallow, eager for quick compliments instead of serious praise?

Henry loped up to them. He jostled Maddie but Nora could tell it wasn't on purpose. Maddie seemed unfazed—it appeared they were all getting used to Henry's puppylike ways and Nora had to admit she was starting to find him endearing.

She wondered about the remark Sasha had made about Henry's father, and the way Henry had reacted—clearly there was a story there. But that would have to wait. "How can you not want a piece of that Astrid glory?" Henry asked her.

"It's not real," Nora said immediately. "I want to be known for investigative reporting, not some frivolous advice column."

"It's not frivolous," Maddie and Jack said in unison, then laughed.

"I don't know what *frivolous* means but it sounds bad, so I agree with them," Henry said firmly.

Now even Nora was laughing.

"It's a smart and fun column that helps people," Maddie insisted. She had pulled off her ponytail holder and was shaking out her smooth, thick hair.

"It's not—" Nora began, but Maddie held up a hand as she interrupted.

"Investigative reporting, but why can't you be known for two things?" Maddie asked. "Can't a girl be serious and fun too?"

"Oh, she dunked on you there, Nora," Henry said cheerfully as they rounded the corner.

Nora could hear the thump of basketballs, the

shouts of players, and laughter. But mostly she was hearing Maddie's words.

"You know Astrid would agree with me," Maddie added, grinning.

Jack nodded before heading into the gym to get Rudy.

Nora had to snicker at that. But also, Maddie had a point—Astrid would never tell a girl she had to be one thing: pretty or smart, into drama or into math. Astrid would say a girl could be many things, that she could be everything. That she should embrace every aspect of herself and her interests with great gusto (Astrid liked to use dramatic words like *gusto*).

"And trust me, Astrid is never wrong," Maddie added.

"But— It's different for you," Nora said, surprised to hear the words come out of her own mouth.

Maddie turned back to Nora, her forehead scrunched. "Why?" she asked.

But then they were interrupted.

"What's up?" a red-faced, disheveled Rudy asked as he and Jack came out of the gym. "Your boy here said it's an emergency."

116

"It is, though we need you to keep it on the down low," Maddie said.

"A stealth operation, I get it," Rudy said, grinning. Nora was glad it was Rudy and not one of his friends who Louis had spoken to. Rudy could be annoying, but guys like Eric and Steve were straight-up obnoxious. They probably wouldn't have even come out to help, and they'd definitely insist on knowing everything.

"We heard you've been talking to Louis," Jack said. Nora noticed he was rubbing his hands on his jeans nervously as he spoke. "We were hoping you could tell us why."

"Sorry, that's classified," Rudy said immediately, and Nora gritted her teeth. Maybe this wasn't going to be so easy.

But then Rudy grinned. "Got you—it's totally not classified. Yeah, Louis and I were chatting recently. What do you want to know?"

"Louis is accused of taking something from Sasha's locker," Jack said, the words rushing together in his obvious relief that Rudy had been kidding. "We need to know why he stole it and we were hoping maybe Louis talked to you about it."

Rudy had stiffened the second Jack said Sasha's name, and Nora found she was holding her breath, waiting for his response. "No," he said shortly, his voice no longer so friendly.

They were onto something, Nora could tell. She stepped forward, her hands held out in what she hoped was a peaceful, diplomatic gesture. "Listen, we don't want to make problems, we just want to help. Louis is in major trouble over this."

Rudy let out a breath that hissed through his teeth. "Yeah, if it involves Sasha, I'm sure he's in trouble."

Henry was frowning. "I thought you and Sasha were friends," he said. He'd been tugging on his hair so much it was standing up straight, giving him a mad-scientist look.

"*Were* being the key word there," Rudy said, glancing into the gym, where Steve, Eric, and Brady seemed to be arguing about something. "She talked some smack about me a few weeks ago and I couldn't care less what she thinks, but that's not a friend move, you know?"

Nora nodded—it was definitely not a friend move.

"But to answer your question, no, Louis wasn't

asking me about Sasha, just about some school stuff," Rudy said.

"He wanted your help?" Henry asked, clearly digging to see if the cheating theory might be true.

Rudy snickered. "No, not at all—that guy doesn't need help with school. He was just asking me about some teachers he never had class with, if they were nice and stuff."

Nora had several questions about that but Jack spoke up.

"We've heard Louis and Sasha talked sometimes and it seemed like they got along," Jack said.

"If Sasha was being nice, she had an angle," Rudy said, shifting his weight from one leg to the other. "That's how she rolls."

"What could her angle be with Louis?" Nora asked, realizing how much she needed—they all needed—Rudy to have an answer.

But Rudy seemed distracted by the argument in the gym that had come to shoves and Coach, who was hustling over. "No idea," he said, shaking his head. "Listen, I need to get back." He started toward the door.

"Wait," Nora said, not caring how desperate she

sounded. "Why did Louis want to know about the teachers?"

But Rudy had already jogged back into the gym.

"Well, that was a lot of nothing," Jack said with a frustrated sigh, leaning against the wall.

Nora wasn't so sure. "Why was he asking if certain teachers were nice?" she muttered. It was a very odd thing to ask about in the middle of November, when the school year had started ages ago.

"Who cares?" Henry said as he paced. "It doesn't have anything to do with Sasha or the backpack, so it doesn't matter. What matters is that we have no idea what Louis is hiding or where to find Sasha's backpack. We're out of leads."

"What about the paper we found in the recycling bin this morning?" Maddie asked. She was twisting her hair band around her fingers so hard it would probably snap soon. "Is it possible we missed something?"

They all looked hopefully at Nora. She could see the paper so clearly in her mind: the two strings of numbers, the wrinkles where it had been folded, the pencil smudges along one side. And absolutely nothing that could help them.

"No," she said ruefully. "I really wish there was."

"You guys don't think there's something to the fact that there were two locker combinations written on it?" Jack asked.

"Nora already said Louis wrote down all the combinations for Sasha that he found when he hacked into the office computer or whatever," Maddie said, with obvious irritation. "Let's not waste time."

"I don't see you coming up with any great ideas," Jack said snippily.

"At least I'm not coming up with bad ones," Maddie retorted.

"You guys are *both* wasting time," Nora could not stop herself from saying. "We have to work together or we're never going to solve this."

"Because we're such a great team?" Jack asked sarcastically. Then he held up a hand. "Sorry, I know, I just—you guys, we have to figure this out. And we're running out of time." His voice was raw, and Nora felt the anxiety she saw in his face fizz up in her own chest. If they didn't get Sasha the backpack—

Maddie was now leaning up against the wall too, her eyes closed, but she nodded. "Okay, you're right, so let's focus," she said. "Who will—"

"Wait!" Henry said so loudly Eric, who was near the door of the gym, glanced out. Henry glanced back, then lowered his voice as the three of them came closer. "You guys, we're not asking the right question: We aren't looking for a who, we're looking for a what."

"What?" Jack asked, confused.

"Exactly," Henry said unhelpfully, nodding. "We don't need to find someone to tell us what's going on. What we need is the backpack. Where is the backpack? That's what we should be asking ourselves."

"But if Principal Montenegro hasn't found it, how are we supposed to?" Maddie asked, though she did look more hopeful.

"We don't know if she's looking for it or just pressuring Louis to say where it is. That's the most likely scenario, because she can't just turn the school upside down if she has no idea where it is," Henry said. He actually sounded like a detective from TV listing clues. "And we can."

"So where should we be looking?" Jack asked.

"What about—" Nora began, but then Maddie broke in.

"At his house," she said, bouncing on her toes. "He wasn't called into Principal Montenegro's office until second period—he could have snuck out this morning, dumped the pack at his house, and then come back."

"Why would he come back?" Nora asked.

"To cover his tracks," Maddie said. "He had no reason to think he'd be caught—he'd done such a good job taking the backpack in the first place."

Henry bit his lip for a moment. "But thanks to us, he *was* caught."

Nora did not like to hear it put that way—they'd had to prove their innocence, after all. But still, Henry's point stung and that was because it was true.

"I'm not sure cutting school and breaking into Louis's house is the best idea," Jack said, frowning.

"No, but we find out if it's at his house by asking Emma," Maddie said. "Remember, she's out of school today."

"Maybe it's not a coincidence that she's absent—maybe she's part of this too!" Henry exclaimed.

Nora was impressed.

"You guys are brilliant," Jack said happily.

"Well, yes," Henry said, grinning. Nora could see how much Jack's remark pleased him.

"I'm going to get Emma's number so we can text her," Maddie called. They all cheered as she raced down the hall toward the dance studio.

CHAPTER 12

MADDIE

There were eight minutes left before lunch ended, so Maddie knew the dance team, whose members had a quick twenty-minute practice after scarfing down their meals, would just be wrapping up. This meant Maddie could easily ask any one of them for Emma's number. Normally a seventh or eighth grader wouldn't have a sixth grader's number in her phone, but being selected for the squad was such an honor that the girls got together on their own to practice too. And to set up those practices, they texted. Unfortunately showing up now also meant that Maddie might run into Coach Faizal, who would definitely be annoyed Maddie hadn't done the write-up yet, but it was obviously a risk Maddie had to take.

Maddie flew around the corner but then stopped abruptly because Ms. Bazile, her math teacher, was walking toward her.

"Not running, are we, Maddie Robinson?" Ms. Bazile asked, smiling.

"Absolutely not," Maddie said, smiling her thanks that Ms. Bazile wasn't getting her in trouble like most teachers would. But Ms. Bazile was someone who actually liked her students. And she was very into math—she had even given Maddie a nickname after Julia Robinson, a famous mathematician. Maddie adored the name, the same way she adored math. And dancing. And a lot of other stuff. Which was why it was so weird to her that Nora was obsessed with being one way. Well, being *seen* as being one way—in reality she was more, everyone was. So what was the big deal? Nora had said it was "different" for Maddie—but why? That was something Maddie definitely planned to follow up on once they'd found the backpack and prevented their lives from disintegrating. That and what Henry and Jack were both hiding. Really there was a lot to uncover today. But first things first.

Ms. Bazile passed and Maddie walked—speedily— toward the dance studio. As she rounded the last corner, she could hear the thump of the bass and Coach Faizal calling out encouragement. She lurked just outside as the song ended and Coach Faizal gave her end-of-practice pep talk while the dancers cooled down.

"Hey, Maddie," Michelle B. said suddenly, surprising Maddie and causing her to leap into the air and shriek. "Whoa, sorry, I didn't mean to scare you."

Maddie laughed at her own over-the-top reaction. "It's not your fault—I'm just a little high-strung today."

"Like Mitten," Michelle B. said knowingly. Her cat Mitten was famous for his extremely sensitive nature. Maddie wasn't super into cats but she had a soft spot for Mitten, who would scuttle wildly from the room in terror if you set down a glass too hard. Yes, Maddie definitely felt like Mitten today.

The door to the studio opened.

"I've got to talk to Coach before class," Michelle B. said, slipping inside. "See you later."

Maddie waved, glad that Michelle B. would be distracting the coach from noticing Maddie's presence. Though she stood a few feet away from the room just in case.

"Hey," she said as Kiara and Jade, two of the dancers, both seventh graders like Maddie, came out, dripping with sweat and glowing from the workout.

"Do either of you guys have Emma's number? I have to ask her something."

They both nodded. "I'll text it to you from the locker room," Kiara said, reaching up to loosen the tight ponytail they all had to wear for dance (except for Jade, who had short hair).

"Thanks," Maddie said, joining them in the short walk from the studio to the lockers. She glanced into the studio as they passed, then stopped suddenly and grabbed Jade's arm. "Why is Sasha practicing with you guys?" she hissed.

Jade politely refrained from asking why Maddie had her elbow in a death grip, and just scowled. "Emma dropped out and Sasha's first alternate."

Maddie had never hyperventilated but she had the feeling she was about to. She pressed two hands on her belly to try and stay calm, then spoke. "Why did Emma drop out?"

Kiara and Jade exchanged a look.

"No one knows," Kiara said.

"Yeah, it was weird because Emma was the only sixth grader to make it and she was super psyched," Jade added as they began walking again, Maddie still pressing her hands on her stomach and taking deep breaths to keep from flipping out.

"But she hasn't been at practice all week and this morning Coach told us she wasn't coming back. Sasha was already practicing with us and now she's part of the squad," Kiara said sourly.

"And acting like she's the assistant coach, telling the rest of us what to do," Jade said, rolling her eyes.

They'd reached the locker room and Maddie knew she had to let them get dressed for class, so she quickly asked her one last question. "Emma didn't drop out because of an injury or something like that?"

"No, Coach said it was for personal reasons," Jade said, pulling open the door for Kiara, who headed inside. "And Coach seemed confused by it too. I bet in the entire history of the Gala no dance squad member ever dropped out—even if they *were* injured."

She had a point—making Gala dance squad was just that special.

"Also," Kiara said, popping out again, "no one's been able to get Emma to text back. We even tried calling her, and nothing. So I'll give you her number but don't be surprised if she doesn't respond."

Maddie raced to Nora, Jack, and Henry, the pieces of the puzzle falling into place so fast her brain was practically humming. It all made sense: Louis breaking into Sasha's locker, his refusal to turn over the backpack, Sasha's determination to get it back—it all fit.

The three were where Maddie had left them, talking in a tight circle outside the gym. "You guys," Maddie said as she ran up, "I know why Louis broke into Sasha's locker!"

And then the bell ending lunch rang.

"We can't talk here," Henry said. They could already hear the cafeteria doors opening and the resulting stampede to get to class.

"Let's go back to the room," Nora suggested. She led the way, Henry, Maddie, and Jack in her wake. Maddie was impressed by how Nora navigated her way and had them back in room 122 in less than a minute, despite the packed hallway.

Henry shut the door and then they all turned to Maddie.

"Okay," she began, sitting down and reminding herself to breathe so she could explain it all without near hyperventilation. "Emma dropped out of the Gala dance squad . . . and guess who the alternate was."

"No!" Nora gasped, getting it immediately.

The boys looked at each other, then at Maddie.

"Sasha," Maddie said. "Sasha is replacing Emma in the Gala."

Henry's eyes opened comically wide and Jack's mouth fell open.

"No way," Henry said breathlessly. "So Sasha found out something about Emma, something she was ashamed of or didn't want made public—"

"And blackmailed her into giving up her spot on the Gala squad!" Maddie finished triumphantly. "The same way she's blackmailing us and who knows how many other people."

"So Louis stole the backpack because it has Emma's secret inside?" Nora asked thoughtfully.

"Looks like it," Maddie said.

"He's a good brother," Jack said.

Nora poked him. "So are you," she pointed out, and Jack smiled.

Henry sat down and rubbed his hands together. "I am too, just for the record," he said. "You should see me crushing it when I play 'The Scary Monster Is Coming,' but let's stay focused," he added. Maddie could not deny being charmed by this, and she had a feeling that Jack and Nora, who were both grinning, felt the same. She was also glad that Jack and Henry seemed to have gotten over their problems and were working together.

"Now we know why Louis risked everything to break into Sasha's locker. We were right—there was totally more to the story," Henry said.

Maddie nodded—they *had* been right. "Why wouldn't Louis just turn the evidence in to Principal Montenegro, to get Sasha in trouble and to save himself and Emma?" Jack asked. He had pulled out his pencils and was rubbing one absently between his palms. "It's not like the principal would tell anyone Emma's secret."

"They're scared Sasha would know they were the ones who turned her in," Henry said. "Can you imagine how miserable Sasha'd make them if they got her in trouble like that?"

"Oh yeah, of course," Jack said, sounding slightly embarrassed he hadn't thought of that himself.

The one-minute bell rang for fifth period.

Henry leaned forward. "We're not leaving here, right?" he asked urgently. "We can't afford to waste any more time."

Even Nora shook her head. "We're here till we figure out where that backpack is. But I am wondering about something else—would Louis really do this for his sister? I mean, being a good brother is one thing, but to risk expulsion to keep something of hers private?"

Maddie was suddenly unsure—that did seem like a huge thing to do for a sister. Not that she had one but still, did brothers do stuff like that?

"Yes," Jack said quietly. "If it would ruin her life."

"Could something Sasha knows genuinely ruin someone's entire life?" Nora asked, now sounding skeptical. "I mean, I don't want her to tell about Astrid, but it wouldn't destroy me or anything."

Maddie had to admit the same was true for her—yes, it would make big problems for Maddie if Coach Faizal saw the video. But Coach was fair—it's not like she'd toss Maddie off dance for life. Maddie would be in trouble, but she'd get some kind of consequence, deal with it, and move on.

Then she saw Jack was nodding, his eyes sad. "If Sasha actually tries to tell people about Matt"—he paused and looked around, then took a breath—"that Matt is bipolar and on medication, it could jeopardize his future in both college and the pros, which means everything to him. So yeah, I'd get expelled to stop her."

Jack had told them his secret—he trusted them that much.

Maddie reached across the table and put her hand on his arm. "Well, we'll keep Matt's secret and we'll get expelled with you if she tells anyone."

"Yup," Nora agreed staunchly. But then she frowned. "We're not doing anything drastic enough to get expelled though, right?"

Henry laughed while Maddie shook her head. Then she looked at Jack. "But we do have his back. And yours."

Jack nodded back. "Thanks," he said, looking at all of them.

Maddie pulled out her phone and looked at the screen. "Okay, Kiara sent me Emma's number, but she warned me Emma might not respond. I'll text her now but we need a backup plan." She clicked on Emma's number and opened a fresh text.

"Do we think Louis spilled Emma's secret to Sasha when they were talking?" Nora asked. "Rudy said if

Sasha was talking to Louis, she had an angle—maybe it was to find out something about Emma."

"But would Louis have told?" Jack said, sounding doubtful. "I'd never let my brother's illness slip."

"It could have been a mistake," Henry said, so roughly Maddie almost dropped her phone. All three of them looked at him. Henry stared down at his hands, which were balled up in his lap. "He might not have wanted to hurt her but then he messed up and it was too late to fix it."

Maddie looked first at Nora, then at Jack, and could tell they were thinking what she was: that Henry was talking about something he had done. Something he deeply regretted but could not repair.

"Okay," Nora said gently, "that's a great point. I'd bet that's why Sasha was talking to him, whether she got anything out of it or not."

Maddie nodded, then looked down at her screen. She'd sent the text, but no three dots had appeared. "She's not responding," she announced. "We may be on our own to find the backpack." The words were acid in her mouth because despite all they'd figured out, they still had no idea what Sasha was after. Or where her bag and its contents were.

"Is there anything this information can tell us that we didn't already know?" Henry asked.

It was discouraging that their detective did not have a next step.

"The thing that worries me," Nora said slowly, like she didn't want to put the thought into the room but had to, "is that Sasha must have been looking for her bag all day, and if she hasn't found it, why would we? I mean, what do we have that she doesn't already know?"

Maddie blinked as a heavy fog of silence filled the room, her eyes teary. Nora was right and—

"There *is* something we have that she doesn't," Jack said, his eyes lighting up.

They all looked at him.

"That second locker combination on the paper we found—what if . . . what if it's not Sasha's from last year?" Jack said. "What if it's *Emma's*?"

Maddie's jaw dropped open.

"Now we know that Louis didn't steal the backpack for himself, he stole it for Emma. So, what if he put it in her locker so Emma could decide what she wanted to do with it."

Of course! That made all the sense in the world!

"So what we need to do is get that backpack, get what's inside, and then decide our next move," Nora said.

"We're going to save us all," Henry said gleefully, making Maddie laugh.

Nora tapped her temple. "I still remember the combination, so let's go see."

But before any of them could respond, someone walked into the room. And Maddie's hopes shattered like a plate dropped from ten stories when she saw who it was.

"Nice work," Sasha said, smoothing back her hair. "You can just give me that locker combination and we'll be done here."

CHAPTER 13

JACK

"No." It was Henry who spoke first.

Jack nodded. They'd come too far to hand over control to Sasha now, before learning what they were actually handing over, when they still had a chance to save Emma and Louis along with themselves. Plus, it suddenly occurred to Jack that giving Sasha what she wanted, without discovering anything about it, left them vulnerable. Because what would prevent Sasha from revealing their secrets the next time she needed their help? No, they needed to know more before giving Sasha what she was after.

"No chance," he added, to make it clear they were in agreement on this. "The only ones opening Emma's locker are the four of us."

"Then let me tell you what's in that backpack, what you think you're protecting, because you doing this, it's not going to change anything about what I know," Sasha said, gliding out the chair at the head of the table and taking a seat like she was running a board meeting.

This seemed unlikely to Jack: Why would Sasha—and Louis, for that matter—go to such extremes over something that wasn't a big deal? And yet the back of his neck prickled, the way it did when he could sense a thunderstorm coming.

"Emma was failing all her classes, so she got tested and diagnosed with a learning disability," Sasha said, like she was reporting a news story. "She had to move to compensatory ed classes last month." She rested her elbows on the table. "Now, I'm not the one who calls CE the stupid classes—I don't judge, that's not who I am." Jack felt his lips curl at this. "But a lot of other people do. Maybe most people in our school, just ask your friend Rudy. He knows all about it because he's in them too—that's how I found out, actually, Louis asking about the classes for his sister. The thing about Rudy though is that he doesn't care. It doesn't matter to him what people think or if they say he's dumb. He's lucky that way. Unlike our friend Emma."

Last August Dad had taken them to Cape Cod

for a week, where they'd eaten way too much at a fried seafood stand. Jack's stomach had been bloated with grease and slippery meat, and that awful feeling, along with a thudding headache, was how he felt right now, hearing Sasha. Because every word she said was true. Some people *did* call those classes the stupid classes—and the people in them dumb. Which infuriated Jack. Dad had a processing disorder, and he was often called "the sharpest mind in college baseball." So yeah, Jack knew learning disabilities had nothing to do with intelligence. It just meant you learned differently, no big thing.

But clearly Emma didn't know that.

"So you have stuff about Emma's learning challenges in your backpack," Maddie said, anger laced through her voice.

"Yes, as a matter of fact I do," Sasha said, gently rubbing the gold bracelet she wore. "Thanks to Louis blabbing to Rudy, I was able to acquire a few things."

"And since you knew she wanted to keep it private, you threatened to tell everyone about it," Henry said, his voice hard as he tugged at his hair yet again. Henry was going to go bald if he wasn't careful.

Sasha shrugged. "I don't care for that word, *threatened*; it's ugly," she said. "But I did say that I'd mention it to people. And Emma knew I had the evidence to prove it."

"You'd share this 'evidence' unless Emma dropped off the Starlight Gala dance squad," Maddie said. "That is just the worst."

Jack nodded at the truth of this, his stomach roiling.

"So apparently you do judge," Sasha said, her tone brittle. "But that Gala performance means more to me than it ever could to Emma. She's in sixth grade, she can do it next year."

"You're in seventh and you have, like, five more years to get chosen," Maddie cried, hands pressed on the table. "And you were the alternate this year—you'd have made it next year for sure!"

"I can't wait till next year," Sasha said sharply. "Someone had to go and it happened to be Emma. Which gets back to my point: I don't need the backpack to let people know what classes Emma's taking. That information's easy to spread regardless."

Jack was puzzled by this—it was true. "Then why do you need it back so badly?" He could tell from the way Nora was leaning forward that she had been wondering the same thing.

And he knew they'd been right not to hand over that locker combination.

"Don't worry about it," Sasha said shortly. "That's not your problem. Your problem is that if you don't give me my bag back, *untouched and unopened*, Emma isn't the only person I'll be talking about."

She stared down her nose, pointedly, at each of them. Jack's hands curled into tight fists. Sasha was threatening Matt—threatening all of them—and that was unacceptable.

"Emma may have a learning disability but she's a smart girl. She knew when to back down," Sasha went on. "I'd advise you to be smart as well."

Henry made a small choking sound and Jack froze, terrified Henry was going to cave. But then Nora spoke up.

"You're right, *threat* is an ugly word," Nora said crisply. Only the pink flushing her cheeks indicated she was anything but relaxed. "That's why it fits: You're threatening us, like you did to Emma. It's definitely ugly and it's definitely not going to work, not this time."

"Maybe you should get some advice from Astrid before you make a final decision," Sasha said. For the first time she sounded flustered. Flustered and angry. "And the good news for you is that she's here in this room with you right now, isn't she, Nora?"

Nora sent Sasha a poison glare so powerful even Jack flinched.

But Sasha simply stood up, smirking. "I told you that you have until the end of the day to get me my backpack and everything inside," she said, "and I honor my word. I just hope you honor the people you should be honoring, and I don't mean Emma." Her eyes met Jack's. "I mean Matt, with that wonderful future he could have ahead of him."

"Don't—" Jack began, leaping up.

But Nora put a hand on his arm and Sasha spoke over him as she headed for the door. "Maddie, I know you don't want Coach Faizal seeing that you called her both stupid and a witch."

"I can't—" Maddie began, her face turning nearly as red as her hair, but Sasha kept going.

"I expect to see all of you at Emma's locker at the end of the day. You can return my untouched possessions then."

"And, Henry—" She'd reached the door but turned with a flourish to deliver one last blow. The blow that Jack sensed would do the most damage. "Do tell your father hello from me. I had such a good meal at Pasta Palace thanks to your dad's service—he's truly an excellent waiter."

And with that she swept out.

"Hold up," Jack said. With all the huge things that had just taken place, he could not wrap his brain around the last words Sasha had said. He had imagined Henry's hidden shame about his father was something like his dad being in the Mafia or wanted by the FBI. Or both. But this? "Your big secret is that your dad . . . works at a restaurant? Why would anyone care about that?"

Henry stood up so fast his chair flew into the wall behind him. "*I* care. I care that people like Sasha and her family treat Dad like he's a loser," he said, each word sizzling hot. "I care that he hates it, that he doesn't make enough money, that he feels ashamed he can't find anything better, and that all of it—*all of it*—is my fault!"

"Okay, got it," Jack said quietly, shrinking down a

bit in his chair. Clearly he hadn't been seeing the full picture. "Sorry."

Henry's eyes were red, though Jack couldn't tell if it was from tears or rage. Or both.

"Let's go to the newspaper office and . . ." Nora started but then trailed off as Henry wrenched open the door.

"I'm done here," he said, and took off down the hall.

"I guess that's my fault," Jack said. It was tough to feel so many things at once: anger, fear, and now guilt. It was making his head hurt.

"No, that was not your fault, that was Sasha's fault," Maddie stormed as she shoved back her chair and rose. "This is all on Sasha, and we need to make it right. And that starts with getting the backpack from Emma's locker—now that Sasha knows where it is, it's not safe. And once we have whatever's inside, we figure out how to stop Sasha from ruining us all."

"Would she know where Emma's locker is?" Nora asked. Then she frowned. "Do we know where it is?"

Maddie nodded. "Yeah, I know—everyone on the team knows that stuff about each other. And Emma's locker is actually right across from Sasha's."

"I don't think Sasha would break into Emma's locker, even if she does know where it is," Jack said, considering. Sasha seemed to prefer letting other people do her hands-on dirty work.

"Then maybe she'll melt off the lock with her evil superpowers," Maddie said, throwing up her hands. "I don't know, I'm just saying I want us to get it."

"Okay, yeah, you're right, let's do it," Jack said, standing up quickly. Who was he to say Sasha didn't have supervillain powers? Which could just be talking her way into getting a custodian to open the locker for her—so why take chances? And who knew what Henry was out there doing? Jack didn't think he'd betray them—and he didn't have the locker combination anyway—but it did seem safest to have the backpack contents in their hands.

Maddie led the way to Emma's locker, going the long way around to avoid passing the office.

"I'll keep lookout," Maddie said when they arrived.

Jack hovered uselessly while Nora spun through the combination. As she moved the dial, it occurred to Jack that he could have made a huge mistake. Maybe the combination wasn't for Emma's locker at all.

Nora tugged at the lock—nothing happened.

It was suddenly hard to pull air into his lungs. Jack braced one hand against the locker next to him to avoid falling over from lack of oxygen.

"Shoot," Nora muttered, spinning through the numbers, this time more slowly.

And then, to Jack's immense relief, the metal door popped open. Nora reached in and pulled out a silver quilted backpack with glitter snaps and a small silver chain on each of the zippers. If this was designer, Jack was not impressed.

"Let's see what we've got here," Nora said, pushing the door shut and heading to the back of the alcove, where passersby would not see them.

Jack and Maddie stood on either side of her, and Nora opened the bag. She rooted around for a moment and pulled out a slim lavender folder. She passed the backpack to Maddie, then opened the folder. A bunch of papers fell all over the floor. Jack quickly knelt down to grab them. Once he had them in a messy pile, he passed them back to Nora, who laid the pile on top of the now-closed folder. They all looked on as Nora slowly leafed through each sheet, and the awful fried-seafood feeling began swirling in Jack's gut again. Here it was, Sasha's evidence: Emma's English essay with red marks all over it, a sheet of math problems with corrections, a science quiz she had failed.

"This makes me so angry," Maddie said, her cheeks pink. "Learning disabilities have nothing to do with how smart you are—they're just about how you learn and that's about teaching, not brainpower. My aunt is dyslexic but she still became a doctor because her professors made sure they taught in ways she could learn and she had the support she needed. And she was top of her class."

Jack nodded vigorously. His dad had a learning difference, as their family called it, so he hated it when people made disparaging and completely clueless remarks about the CE classes.

Nora handed Maddie the work and opened the folder to see the other pages inside. "It's even worse than it looks," she said after a moment. "Sasha somehow stole this from Emma and was going to put it up at the Gala, in the section for best work."

"How do you know?" Henry asked, horrified.

Nora held up one of the papers—it was a flyer for the Gala with a map of each display. Sasha had circled the spot where classwork would be shown, as well as scrawled, "Gala volunteers leave at 5:30 for dinner before the event," next to it. Clearly that was when she planned to sneak in and put up Emma's work—after the volunteers left, when it would be too late for anyone to fix it.

Maddie looked like she too had the fried-seafood feeling. "And she could have done it easily—she'd be allowed in early for dance, so she would have access after the volunteers left, before everyone came."

"If Emma was already feeling embarrassed about her new classes, can you imagine how awful she'd feel having this posted for the whole school to see?" Nora asked, and then, eyes wide, held up a sheet of paper that made Maddie gasp.

There was more in the folder: Emma was not the only person Sasha had dirt on.

"We are not looking at any of these," Nora said, stuffing them back into the folder with such force they crumpled a bit. "This is not information we should know—that *anyone* should know."

All Jack had seen was the name of another Gala dancer, Kiara, and a list beneath it. And Nora was right—that was more than he wanted to see. He did not need private information about Kiara or anyone else. As Nora had said, no one did.

"What do we do with the non-Emma pages?" Maddie asked quietly.

Jack considered this but then realized there really wasn't a choice. "We have to give everyone their pages. They need to know Sasha did this, that she gathered their private information."

Nora was nodding. "I'd want to know."

"Yeah," Maddie agreed, "you're right. I'd want to know, for sure. I can give them back—Kiara's on dance and I'm guessing the others are too. I'll explain and tell them we never read anything past their names."

Nora nodded as she pulled the papers out of the folder and passed them to Maddie, who folded them over tightly and stuck them in her back pocket. She told them she would put them in her bag as soon as she could, to keep them safe.

Nora tucked Emma's papers back in the folder, which she held tight across her chest with both hands.

"No wonder Emma agreed to drop out of the show," Jack said.

"No wonder Louis stole the backpack for her," Nora said.

And that brought Jack up short. Their whole plan was finding the backpack and discovering what was inside it and why Louis had been willing to get expelled to keep it hidden. And why Sasha was so desperate to get it back. They had assumed once they knew that, they'd be able to stop Sasha. But that was not the case.

"You guys, there's no way we can give this stuff back to Sasha," Jack said. "We can't let her have Emma's work or the dirt she's gathered on other people. That would make us accomplices or something—it would mean we knew but let her have it anyway."

"But if we *don't* give it back, Sasha will ruin us," Maddie said, her eyes hard.

"We have to find another way to stop her," Jack said.

"And her reign of tyrannical evil," Maddie muttered.

Jack was really beginning to appreciate Maddie.

"Don't worry, I know how to take down tyrants," Nora said confidently.

The bell rang, ending fifth period, and Jack heard classroom doors bursting open. "How?" he asked as they walked out into the hall, because now they did not have to be concerned someone would see them out of class.

"Research," Nora said. "Of course."

With that she took off toward the newspaper office.

"Research, obviously," Maddie said jokingly to Jack, clearly as confused as he was.

Jack laughed. "Obviously."

And they headed off down the hall after Nora.

CHAPTER 14

NORA

Ms. Holt held her eighth-grade English classes in the room next to the newspaper office, so Nora went there first.

"How's one of my very favorite reporters?" Ms. Holt asked when she saw Nora. Then she scowled at something over Nora's shoulder. "Hey, gentlemen, no throwing objects of any sort. Seats now." A group of boys sheepishly stopped tossing a tennis ball (why did they have a tennis ball? It wasn't even tennis season—boys were weird.) and sat.

Ms. Holt turned back to Nora. "I'm guessing you want to spend the period in the office working on an article?"

One of the many perks of being a staff reporter who got straight As was the option to get a free period in the newspaper office.

"Yes, and Jack is going to help me," Nora said. This was true—she just wasn't going to mention that the help was not newspaper related. "And Maddie Fox is going to work with us, if that's okay. She has gym this period."

"As long as it's okay with Coach, it's fine with me," Ms. Holt said, glancing at the clock. The bell was about to ring.

"Thanks," Nora said, not saying anything about Coach to avoid telling an actual lie. She hurried out into the hall, where Maddie and Jack were waiting. Maddie had Sasha's backpack hidden in her messenger bag, which she'd secured over her shoulder. And the folder was safely stowed in Nora's satchel.

"We're good," Nora said, waving them into the *Sentinel* office as the last straggling students rushed to class.

The newspaper room was Nora's favorite spot in school. It was a double-sized classroom with rows of desks with computers taking up the middle, file cabinets along one wall, and an art table and bookshelf filled with reliable sources and journalism books on the other. Ms. Holt's desk was piled high with papers and pictures of her cat, Tango. And the walls were covered with past front pages, art spreads, and even a few awards. Nora breathed in the scent of paper and pine cleaner, already feeling better. They'd find their answers here, she was sure of it.

Ms. Maxwell, the school aide who supervised the room when Ms. Holt was in class, looked up briefly from the book she was reading. Ms. Maxwell was in law school at night and spent every second she could studying. "Hi, Nora, Jack, and friend," she said cheerily. "Let me know if you need anything."

"Thanks," Nora said. She strategically settled at the computer farthest from Ms. Maxwell, to avoid her overhearing anything.

Maddie and Jack settled down in chairs next to her, Maddie rolling out her neck for a moment. "This has been the most stressful day ever," she said.

"And it could get a lot worse," Jack said. He had pulled his sketch pad out of his bag and was rolling a pencil between his palms. Nora figured he was deciding what to draw or that rolling the pencil soothed him. Or both.

"This is when it gets better," Nora announced. Then she said words she never could have imagined uttering. "I wish Henry was here though."

Jack shook his head. "I can't believe I'm saying this but me too."

"Yeah," Maddie agreed. "It's not the same without the whole team here."

Nora nodded, then flexed her fingers and typed Sasha's full name into the search bar.

"What's the plan?" Maddie asked, focusing on the screen. "Don't waste your time on Sasha's socials. Coach keeps a close eye on all our accounts, so we all just post pictures from dance and pet pics and stuff."

"Then we see what a basic search turns up and go from there," Nora said, taking in the list that had popped up.

"What are we looking for?" Jack asked. He'd begun outlining something on his pad, though Nora couldn't tell what just yet.

"An explanation for why this Gala means so much to Sasha she'd blackmail a teammate for a spot," Nora said, then glanced at Maddie. "Because she's over the top here, right?"

"Totally," Maddie agreed emphatically. "It's a big honor to make the Gala squad but there are other dance events throughout the year."

"So I think our next step is figuring out why Sasha would go to such extremes for this one performance, why it's so important to her," Nora said. She was using what she'd learned from a psychology article she'd read for an Astrid column. Writing Astrid involved a surprising amount of research. "If we understand her motive, maybe we can talk her out of threatening people or help her find a way to get what she wants without bringing down half the school."

"Or figure out a way to make it so she can't get what she wants even if she does bring down half the school," Maddie added.

"Right, the goal is to stop her, and I don't think we can do that until we know what she actually wants," Nora said. "Why she's so incredibly desperate to dance in this Gala."

"Makes sense," Jack said.

"So why is the Gala special?" Nora asked, pausing in her computer search.

"Being chosen means you're one of the very best on the team," Maddie said. "That's something."

Nora nodded. "Anything else?"

"Well, it's being livestreamed on Tansy Mink's YouTube channel. That's a big deal for anyone on a school dance team," Maddie said, twisting a lock of hair.

"How is it a big deal?" Nora asked, leaning forward. "Does it lead to some kind of opportunity for dancing on Broadway or something?"

Maddie shook her head. "No, Tansy Mink's not scouting dancers who can go pro, just showcasing talented school dance teams. It's an ego boost mostly—a big one obviously, but it doesn't impact your life in some major way."

Jack snorted. "Sasha is not seeking an ego boost—she's got plenty of that."

Nora laughed. "Yeah, that's true. But there must be something else she can get from it, right?" She turned back to the computer because she knew the answer lay there, in the search.

Jack continued to sketch as Nora clicked on each link, taking note of what she saw. After a few minutes Maddie seemed bored because she got up to see what Jack was working on.

"That is amazing," she said, and Nora glanced over. Jack was doing a comic-style picture of a dance team performing.

"Seriously, you need to get your dad and brother on board with this," Maddie went on. "How are they not thrilled with what you can do?"

"Okay, so maybe it's possible I haven't exactly shown them much of my stuff," Jack admitted.

Nora stopped her search and spun around. "Why?" both she and Maddie demanded, nearly in unison. Nora looked at Maddie and they smiled.

"It probably sounds stupid, but everyone in my family, not just my dad and brother, and my mom before she died, but my aunts and uncles and cousins—they're sports people," Jack said. "It's who everyone is. Everyone but me."

"So you feel left out?" Maddie asked.

"Maybe, yeah, but it's not just that," Jack said, rolling his pencil between his palms. He bit his lip for a second, and Nora could tell the real story was coming. "It's just—art is kind of wimpy in comparison," he said in a small voice. "Like, they pump iron and trash talk, and I draw pretty pictures of flowers." He said this as though it were something shameful.

"Pretty flowers are hard to draw," Nora said. "They take real skill. I think the problem isn't that they'd think it's wimpy—it's that you think it's wimpy. And so *you're* not proud of it."

Jack appeared to consider her words as Maddie smirked.

"Astrid comes through again," she said.

Nora lifted an eyebrow at this, but she had to admit it felt good to give advice. Was it possible that was part of why she'd started the column? But there was no time to mull this over because as it happened, she had more to say.

"If you acted like everything you drew—flowers, portraits, whatever—was as cool as a home run, they'd be cheering you on," she continued. "Unless they're all jerks, but from what you've told us, I'm pretty sure they aren't."

"No, they aren't," he said. He seemed very certain of this and Nora was glad. Jack was kind and deserved a kind family.

"You know what you need to do?" a familiar voice called.

Nora saw Maddie's grin and knew the one spreading over her face matched. Henry loped in puppylike, his hair standing up as usual. Even Jack was smiling.

"You need to draw baseball pictures," Henry said.

Jack's brows drew together for a moment as he thought about it. "That's not a half-bad idea actually," he said.

"It's brilliant," Henry said, pulling a chair over to sit with them.

"New person who has come into the newspaper office, you have permission to be here, correct?" Ms. Maxwell called.

"Absolutely," Henry said with a salute.

Ms. Maxwell smiled. "Good."

"So what are we doing?" Henry asked. "Besides telling Jack to accept that he's a wimp."

Jack snorted as Maddie rolled her eyes. But they were both smiling.

"See, Nora, look at me: funny, smart, and the best-looking guy in school," Henry declared. "I am many things and you can be too."

Nora was detecting something under Henry's bravado, something closed off, protected. And for the first time it occurred to her to wonder why Henry joked around all the time. Still, she wouldn't bring up his secret until he did.

"He's right, Nora," Maddie said. "And finish what you were saying before, about how it's different for you."

Nora did not especially feel like discussing this,

but she'd brought it upon herself, so there was no trying to get out of it. "I'm short," she said.

The other three seemed to be waiting for more.

"That's it?" Maddie asked after a moment.

"Yup," Nora said, going back to the computer and scrolling down the page she'd discovered.

"We know you're short," Jack said, a bit too bluntly for Nora's taste. "So what?"

"So when you're as short as I am and *cute*," Nora spat out the hated word, "no one takes you seriously."

"Everyone takes you seriously," Henry said, glancing at the others. "Right?"

"Totally," Jack agreed.

But Maddie took a moment to respond. "So you think if you're anything besides this super hard-core reporter girl who never smiles and carries an, ah, *odd* bag—"

"My satchel is not odd!" Nora exclaimed indignantly.

"It's called a satchel. It's odd," Jack said definitively.

"That's not even a conversation," Henry said in a *duh* voice.

"Whatever," Nora said, and rolled her eyes, though she couldn't help grinning a little. She wasn't used to being teased by friends and realized she kind of liked it.

"And if people find out you are more than just a flinty reporter, that you write the funnest column in the paper—"

"The fluffiest," Nora corrected.

"So if you write something besides boring stories about the city council"—Nora squeaked indignantly at this—"people will stop taking you seriously?" Maddie asked. "*This* is what you believe?"

"It sounds kind of stupid when you say it like that, but trust me, I've been talked down to way too many times to risk letting people know I write Astrid," Nora said, not allowing herself to think about that warm proud feeling she'd gotten earlier. Or her pleasure at giving useful advice.

"It sounds stupid because it is stupid," Maddie said.

Henry laughed and reached out for a high five, which Maddie gave with gusto. Nora was irritated with them both.

"You're the only one who thinks Astrid is fluff," Jack said. He'd started a new drawing, though Nora couldn't tell what it was yet.

"Plus you love that column and you're proud of it,"

Maddie said. She held up her palms before Nora could protest. "I can tell, so don't bother denying it."

Nora was rattled that Maddie could read her so well. She'd barely allowed herself to feel that pride— and Maddie had seen it?

"You're worried you're fluffy and Jack's worried he's a wimp and I think you just both need to get over yourselves and embrace the things you love to do," Henry said calmly.

They all turned to him and he shrugged. "What? I read it in an Astrid letter and it seemed pretty smart to me."

Nora had to laugh as she turned back to the computer. She did not like the fact that what they were saying made sense. A lot of sense. Had she gotten it wrong? Would she still be respected if she was known as a flinty reporter *and* as Astrid? Who really was rather quick-witted and insightful. A good listener and never, ever judgmental. It was something to think about. But not right now, when the clock was ticking.

"Okay, we need to focus," she said, going back to her screen.

Jack continued to draw while Henry settled into

the seat next to him and Maddie wandered over to the art desk.

"I think I found something," Nora announced a minute later.

The three of them crowded so close Nora could no longer type.

"What?" Maddie asked breathlessly.

"That's just Sasha's mom's old-person social media page," Henry said, taking it in. "How's that helpful?"

"It tells us several things," Nora said happily, poking out her elbows so they'd give her space to maneuver. "First, the early posts are all about Sasha dancing in recitals and school shows and stuff. And then they stop. Suddenly."

"Does that mean Sasha stopped dancing?" Maddie asked, sounding surprised.

"It seems like there's a gap," Nora explained, scrolling back up. "In the six months before they moved to Snow Valley, there are zero Sasha dance pictures. But they started up again as soon as she joined the team here."

"Interesting," Maddie said thoughtfully.

"So how do we find out why she stopped performing during that time?" Jack asked.

"I have a lead on that," she said. "Because this account also tells us where Sasha used to live."

"In the Village of Supervillains?" Henry asked.

Jack snickered appreciatively.

"Upstate, in Troy," Nora said. "And you can see from her dance team uniform she went to Oak Ridge Elementary."

"This is a nice tour of her life," Henry said in a way that made it clear he thought it anything but nice, "but so what? And who cares?" He was tugging at his hair again.

"This is how research works, it's slow," Nora said. She ignored Henry (who muttered, "Because it's boring") and continued. "So now we look for pictures with other people from the school, to see if Sasha has a bestie who—"

"No one says *bestie* anymore," Maddie said gently, patting Nora's knee.

"You guys have to stop interrupting," Nora said, exasperated. "Go away, I'm not getting anything done with you badgering me." Nora was not pleased to hear how much she sounded like her mother. But really, how could she get anything done with all these questions? (Which was what her mother had said just last night when Nora tried to interview her for an article on waste management in Snow Valley.)

"Fine, geez," Henry huffed, standing up and beginning to pace. He was doing the thing Nora's favorite little cousins, Betsy and Laura, did of touching anything they passed and picking things up for no reason, always getting sticky fingerprints on everything. Betsy and Laura were three and five, so they had an excuse, but Henry did not. Nora would mention this issue to him later, but for now she focused.

She looked at a series of pictures Sasha's mom had taken of the dance team and noted the other parents tagged who were making comments. (None of the girls were tagged, meaning they probably didn't have accounts. Henry was right about it being for old people.) While Sasha did not seem to have a bestie (why had that word been retired? It was a good word.), she was generally standing next to the same three girls, so Nora compared pictures and then got on their moms' pages. Then, armed with their names, she was ready. She went to the Oak Ridge Middle School page, then logged in to the new middle school Socially Safe site on her own account to send a message. Socially Safe was the pilot social media site most schools in New

York State were using, and luckily Oak Ridge was one of them.

"Okay, it's time," she announced. Henry and Maddie hurried to sit next to her, and Jack looked up from his drawing. "I'm going to message three of Sasha's old teammates to see what they know about her break from dancing."

"Why does it matter?" Henry asked.

"Because it's weird," Nora said. "And when something's weird, there's usually more to it. So if we find out what it is, we might also find out why Sasha is so obsessed with the Gala, why she's threatening everyone, and how to stop her."

"Wow, that's pretty impressive," Henry said.

Nora looked up, gratified. "That's the power of research."

"It's still boring," Henry said. Then he saw Nora's glare. "But really great. Super great. The greatest."

Nora nodded, then gave Maddie her full attention. "Do you want to write the email?"

Maddie looked horrified. "Why would I get near a keyboard when Astrid is here?"

Nora had to chuckle at that.

"Do your magic," Henry added.

Nora thought for a moment, then typed:

> Hi, I saw your dance videos and you are awesome!! And you used to dance with a girl who's now at our school in Snow Valley, Sasha Saturday. She's on the team with me and it seems like she might be hiding something. We don't want her messing anything up for us. You seem like the kind of person who knows it all—details please!!!

"Nice," Maddie said as Nora pressed send, hoping that Geneva Jones would see this and respond. Just in case, she started a new message to the second girl from the site, Cleo Rivera.

"Does this mean Astrid is allowed to use *bestie*?" Nora asked. She was joking—Astrid never used old-school slang.

"No one is allowed to say that word," Maddie declared.

Nora pressed send on Cleo's email, and was about to start a message to the third girl, Lila Thompson, when her in-box pinged.

"That was fast," Henry said. He'd stood up to wander and touch things more but hurried back as Nora opened the message. And then there was silence as they took in what Geneva had written in response:

Did you know Sasha's mom is a criminal?

CHAPTER 15

HENRY

Long before Henry had ruined everything for his family, before Covid had crippled the town and started the downslide of Henry's life, Henry had been pretty quick to judge people. It wasn't something he was aware of, it was just how he thought about things. Like when Mr. Prince, who lived in the house across the street, screamed at Henry for running into his yard after a rogue soccer ball, Henry decided Mr. Prince was a jerk. Or when Todd, a boy a year ahead of them, tried to punch Nathan for accidentally bumping into Todd in the hall, Henry had referred to Todd as a volatile bully. And when his uncle Pete's gambling debts caused Pete and his then wife to lose their house, Henry wrote his uncle off as a loser. But then when Covid hit and Coach House, the restaurant Dad had started with his best friend, Mohammad, before Henry was born, went under, it all changed. Mohammad moved to Maine and Dad began spending most of the day in bed. He cooked and cleaned while Mom worked clerking at the pharmacy, then went to lie down. No matter what time it was or how long he'd been up, he'd go back to the bedroom as soon as he'd completed a task. Henry spent the long days of lockdown and online school helping his brother and sister, and staring at that closed bedroom door.

Mom assured them that Dad's "spirits would pick up" when he could start work again. But there was a new wrinkle between her brows, born of the pandemic, and it deepened every time she said this. So Henry wasn't super surprised when vaccinations slowly allowed the world to open but Dad still stayed in bed. Henry heard what people like Mom's best friend, Ramona, said about Dad, that he was lazy and dumping everything on Mom. But they didn't see how sad Dad was. They didn't understand that Coach House had been Dad's life, the thing that made him happy. That without Coach House Dad just didn't see much reason to get out of bed.

Which was when Henry realized he'd been judgmental like that too. Maybe Mr. Prince screamed that day because something really sad had happened to him, like his fish died. Maybe Todd struggled to control his temper and later felt awful he'd almost hit Nathan. And maybe Pete's gambling was, as Mom had said, an illness. Or maybe not. The point was, Henry had no idea. He didn't know their stories, just like no one knew Dad's. That was when Henry stopped judging.

And that was why he was now disgusted by Geneva telling a bunch of random strangers something that might be a fact but also might not. People were accused of a lot of things, but that didn't mean they'd done them. Had Geneva spoken to Sasha's mom, done research, Nora style, to get the background to fully understand what had happened, if an actual crime had taken place? Because unless she had, Geneva had no business sharing that information—she was just judging. And Henry was worried that Maddie, Nora, and Jack would do the same. After all, if Dad hadn't fallen to pieces, Henry would be right there judging with them.

"What do you think her mom did?" Nora asked, sounding both curious and concerned.

Henry's stomach knotted. Who cared what she might have done? It wasn't their business.

"It's got to be pretty serious if she's an actual criminal," Jack said, biting at a cuticle.

What, so now Jack was an expert on the criminal justice system? Henry's gut twisted up even tighter.

"Do you think she's dangerous?" Maddie asked. "She could be a murderer or—"

"Stop!" Henry exclaimed, slapping a hand down on the table.

"Are we okay over there?" Ms. Maxwell asked. She closed her book, her full attention on them.

"Fine, sorry," Nora called back quickly. But her eyes were on Henry. "What's up?" she asked him quietly.

Henry let out a shaky breath. Instead of pointing out he'd messed up or getting mad at him, she was actually wondering why he had yelled. She might be judging Sasha's mom but she wasn't judging Henry. This was so unexpected, and so kind, that Henry let words tumble out unchecked.

"We don't know anything about Sasha's mom," he said. "People always think they know my dad's story, that he was a failure or that he gave up when he lost his restaurant or that he doesn't care about us because he's sad, like really, *really* sad. But it's not his fault—he didn't ask for a pandemic to close his restaurant or his partner to leave town, and when things opened up, he tried to get a good job, and he would have gotten it too if it weren't for—" Henry finally managed to make his mouth stop talking because what was he doing pouring this out?

But of course it was too late; he'd messed up yet again. One look at Nora told him that she knew what he had managed not to say.

"You think it's your fault your dad didn't get the job," she said.

Was it strange that hearing her say his biggest shame out loud was almost a relief, like something trapped in a closet finally set free? Because it should have made him angry, yet instead his shoulders loosened and a hard place in his chest opened up, just a little.

"It's not something I *think*," Henry said. "It's just how it is." And since he'd gone this far, he figured he might as well let them know what a bad guy he truly was. "My dad applied for the manager job at Frank and Sally's, right when they were hiring staff and getting ready to open."

A couple from New York City had moved to Snow Valley during the pandemic and opened an upscale new restaurant, Frank and Sally's, in a Victorian house they'd had remodeled. It was fancier than Coach

House but had the same kind of American food that Dad knew well: steak, fish, fresh pork chops, and local specialties like corn hash and pies made with apples from the orchard outside town. Dad was a shoo-in for the job, the most qualified person around.

"He was happy when they called him in for an interview," Henry said. "Like, he started getting out of bed more and talking a little about some of the stuff he'd do if he got the job." Dad actually hadn't gotten out of bed that much more, but the family was confident he would once he'd nailed down the job. "But, yeah, you can probably guess that I made Dad miss the interview, so he lost the job. I was supposed to watch Lacey and George because Mom was at work, but I was biking with friends and I lost track of time and ruined Dad's shot at the job."

He decided not to add that Dad had barely been out of bed since. But thinking about it—and saying out loud what he had done—was making his eyes kind of watery and there was a scratchy place in his throat.

"Henry, I don't think—" Maddie began, but just then, to Henry's great relief, Nora's Socially Safe account pinged with a new message.

"We can talk about it later," Henry said (by which

he meant never). "We need to save Louis and Emma and us."

Maddie looked at him carefully for a moment, then nodded. When they all leaned over the computer screen, Henry took a quick moment to swipe his eyes.

"Whoa," Nora, who finished reading first, said.

As Henry kept reading, it was clear the message was indeed a "whoa."

When Sasha's mom came to town, she beat out all the candidates for the curator job at Luscious Gallery. That job was supposed to go to my mom, but don't worry, she has it now. Then Mrs. Saturday started taking over everything, from the PTA to the town council. She was too good to be true, that's what everyone said. So my mom did something about it: She hired an investigator and it turned out Sasha's mom totally lied about her past!!! She was convicted of stealing from her job when she was twenty-three!!!!! And when she applied for the Luscious job, she LIED about it!!!!! So my mom saved us all because OMG, Mrs. Saturday had committed an actual crime!! My mom made sure EVERYONE knew the truth. The dance coach tried to keep Sasha on the team but none of us wanted a convict's daughter in our locker room!!! We had to push but we got her to quit. And you should too!!! Be careful—she tried to cyberbully me after that, but my mom got the police on it and she was suspended and then left for good. TG!!!!!

"I think Sasha learned her bullying tactics from Geneva," Maddie said, disgust laced through each word.

"And her mother," Nora added, her lips pursed. "I can't believe her mom actually hired an investigator. And they had no right to tell everyone—I think that might even be illegal."

"It should be," Henry said. "If she was a serial killer on the loose, then you'd have to tell people, but what, they were worried she'd fake an application for the dance team?"

"Seriously," Jack said, his nose wrinkled.

Nora's computer notified them that another message had come in.

"I don't even want to know what she's saying now," Maddie said, pushing her chair back. "Geneva is solid mean."

"Actually this one is from Cleo, another girl on the

team," Nora said, opening it. Maddie moved closer as once again they all leaned over Nora's screen.

Sasha's mom had some legal problems when she was young. Some people found out and basically pushed Sasha off the team. Sasha was the lead dancer and a lot of people wanted that role. That was part of it too. It got ugly. Sasha was really bitter—the team was her life and she loved being the best. Then she got in all this trouble at school for cyberbullying and was suspended. It was bad. I think her family moved because of it. I would have moved to a cave if it had happened to me.

"Yikes," Maddie said. "Major drama."

"With major blackmail and threats," Nora said, grimacing. "Now we know where Sasha learned how to play this game so well."

"If she got kicked off her old team for being too bossy, why isn't she chilling out here?" Jack asked. He sketched as he spoke, but Henry couldn't tell what this new drawing was yet. "And, Maddie, you said it's not that big a deal to be in the Gala, so why did Sasha go all out with her threats over it? Didn't she learn anything at her old school?"

This was a good question. If Sasha hadn't been picked for the school dance team at all, maybe this would make more sense, but why risk getting tossed off again for one night, one performance, when she had so many others? Why go nuclear about it? Plus, you'd think after having an awful experience on her old team—that had maybe even driven their family out of town—she'd have picked a new hobby altogether.

Nora was looking at Maddie. "You said what makes the Gala dancers special is that the chosen dancers know they're the best—maybe she did need to prove she was the best after getting driven off her old team."

Maddie chewed on her lip for a moment, then shook her head. "I guess . . . but you're the best if you get picked from tryouts. Taking over for someone doesn't change that she's still the alternate, you know?" She looked at Cleo's email again. "Here Cleo says Sasha was bitter—you know what I think?"

"That anyone would be bitter if one of their teammates exposed their family's secrets and chased them out of the city?" Henry asked. It seemed pretty obvious to him.

"Well, yeah, that, but I think Cleo also might mean Sasha was bitter at her old school when she couldn't show off how she was the best, because she wasn't on the team anymore." Maddie was absently twirling a lock of hair and speaking slowly, as if she was working this out as she spoke. "And, sure, she made the team here, but it's not like her old teammates know that or see her star shining or whatever—"

Nora clapped her hands and there was suddenly something in the air, a small current of electricity crackling around them. "Maddie, that's it! Sasha needed to perform in the Gala because it's on Tansy Mink's YouTube channel, so all her old teammates will see she really is the best!"

Well, that made sense too. A lot of sense actually. In fact—it was brilliant.

"Yeah, that's what I meant," Maddie said, grinning.

Henry grinned back. "You have the makings of a real detective," he said.

"Okay," Nora said, rubbing her hands. "Now we know why Sasha wants this so much. She needed to show off to her old team, to let them know she just got bigger and better after they drove her out of town. We have her motive!"

"Which means now we're the ones with power," Jack said. He stopped sketching and was bobbing a bit in his chair. "Because this is information she would obviously never want made public, kind of like all the information she has on us and Emma. We finally have some leverage."

Henry had not thought this far but Jack was right: They finally had some skin in the game, as his gambling uncle Pete would say.

"So the question is," Jack went on, "what should we do now?"

CHAPTER 16

MADDIE

Henry steepled his fingers and raised an eyebrow, looking a lot like an archvillain from a movie. "I say we make her suffer and beg for mercy," he said gleefully.

Nora rolled her eyes. "Or we can be normal people and threaten her for a change, till she backs down."

"That's not as fun," Henry said sulkily. But Maddie saw how his eyes were shining and he was smiling. He was relieved, he pretty much radiated it. Nora had lost the tightness around her mouth that Maddie hadn't even noticed was there until now, when it was gone. And Jack was smiling at Henry, his whole body relaxed. Because they were going to win this face-off with Sasha. And that was a good thing. Great, even. Maddie knew all this.

So why wasn't *she* feeling good?

Jack walked over to a mailbox area, where all the newspaper staff had slots, and slipped his drawing inside his box for storage.

"You should finish that, it's good," Henry said.

Jack grinned. "I will," he said. "But later—the bell's about to ring and I think we need to go to seventh period—I do anyway—so we should figure out where to find Sasha."

Maddie glanced at the clock and realized Jack was right. And there was no way she could be late for science, which was across the school and the class she had next. Mr. Jenkins said lateness was an automatic detention, which would mean missing dance team practice. There was no way Maddie could risk that, considering she was already on thin ice with Coach Faizal. "I have to rush if I'm going to make it to the lab," she said. "Can we find Sasha later?"

"You want to postpone our moment of victory?" Henry asked with exaggerated disbelief.

Maddie was starting to find him irritating again.

"We don't have time to find her before last period anyway," Nora said, pulling her satchel (which really was odd) over one shoulder. "Let's just do what she said and meet her at Emma's locker after the last bell."

"They do say revenge is a dish best served cold," Henry said as they all headed for the door.

"What does that mean?" Jack said, jovial as can be. "You don't eat it."

Clearly he didn't find Henry annoying at all. Even Nora was grinning.

"That is an excellent point," Henry said happily.

Maddie tried to tamp down her annoyance with Henry. It wasn't his fault she was suddenly crabby for no apparent reason. And hearing Henry's story had changed how she thought about him. This whole day had, really. It was like when you got a pop-up book and at first the page stayed flat, but then as you cracked the book open, the full 3D image sprang to life. Henry had always seemed like a clown, shallow and silly. But it turned out he was an older brother with a huge amount of responsibility in a family that was struggling around money, with a dad who—well, Maddie had a lot to say about Henry's dad. And she planned to say it all once the whole Sasha mess had been cleared up. But she got why Henry was such a doofus in school: because here he could be a kid and at home he was one of the adults. And that was not an easy thing when you were twelve and a big goofy puppy like Henry.

"Okay, so we meet at Emma's locker right after school?" Jack confirmed.

The bell was ringing for the end of sixth period, so they headed out of the newspaper office.

"Let's get to Emma's locker fast," Nora said. "We're going to need a few minutes to come up with a game plan before we confront Sasha."

"See you there," Maddie agreed. Then she picked up her pace, to be sure she made it to science on time.

"Hey, Maddie," Debbi, one of Maddie's closest friends, called, squeezing past two eighth-grade girls to catch up with Maddie. She was also in science this period and Maddie was happy to see her.

"How's it going?" Debbi asked, falling in step with Maddie. She had black hair with one lock of bright pink that she tucked behind her ear as they walked.

"It's been a really strange day," Maddie said. They were passing the alcove with Emma's locker, and Maddie stumbled slightly.

"Yeah?" Debbi asked.

Kiara passed and she and Maddie waved at each other.

"Yeah," Maddie said, deciding she could share a

little with Debbi and then ask for her advice. Debbi gave excellent advice. Almost as good as Astrid's.

"It's about Sasha," Maddie said, glancing around to make sure neither Sasha nor any of her friends were nearby. "And something she's doing to someone that's really not okay, but I just—" Maddie realized there was no way to continue without giving away something she should not give away. "Actually forget it," she said.

They were near the lab and the hall was clearing—the bell would ring soon.

"Listen," Debbi said quietly, "my mom is friends with her mom, and I totally get how mean Sasha can be—she's the last person I'd ever want to hang out with."

Maddie was really surprised by this. Well, not that Debbi wouldn't hang out with Sasha—none of Maddie's friends were into that kind of power-play popularity. Or hanging out with mean people. But she was surprised that Debbi's mom, who definitely qualified as a nice mom, was friends with Sasha's mom. Was it possible Sasha had a nice mom?

"They've been through some stuff and I think it's made Sasha hard—the kind of person who doesn't really trust anyone," Debbi said.

They arrived at the lab just as the bell rang, and Maddie hurried to her seat, which was two tables down from Debbi's.

"All right, folks, notebooks out," Mr. Jenkins said from his desk, where he was taking roll. An icy finger slid down Maddie's back as she remembered the morning's close call with him. "In a moment I will begin today's lecture on the water cycle. Make sure you write everything down—you will need it for tomorrow's lab." His eyes flicked from the students to his desk as he checked off attendance.

Maddie's science notebook was in her locker—she'd forgotten to get it. Ian, who sat next to her, noticed and silently passed her a sheet of paper and a spare pencil. Maddie smiled her thanks, then got ready to focus on what would undoubtedly be a very boring set of facts. Not that she was interested in the water cycle under the best of circumstances, but Mr. Jenkins could make anything dull.

As her teacher began to drone, Maddie could not concentrate. She kept thinking about what Debbi had said, what Geneva had shared—and the *way* she'd shared, gleeful in her takedown of Sasha. Exhilarated by the fact that the great Sasha had fallen, and fallen hard. And then there was the thing Cleo had said: "It got ugly." Maddie had a feeling Sasha had always been competitive, invested in being the best and being popular. But what she had been through at her old school would make that even more essential here. Because now she had something to prove. And it must've been horrible to have her mom destroyed like that. That probably counted as an actual trauma. Of course Sasha was hard. Of course she didn't trust anyone.

And now Maddie, Jack, Henry, and Nora were going to make it worse. They were going to make Sasha revisit the worst time of her life with more threats. They were going to hurt her more. Which made them as bad as Geneva. Except—except if they didn't, Sasha would get away with stealing Emma's spot. She would succeed in her threats to Maddie, Nora, Jack, and Henry. And she would always have that information at her fingertips, ready to use if she deemed it necessary.

". . . next in the process is precipitation, otherwise known as . . ."

Maddie wrote this down, even though it made little sense since she had missed what had come before. She wanted to do well on the lab. Maddie liked getting good grades and she didn't want to lose her high score in this class. But her mind kept slipping back to Sasha, Louis, Emma, and the dilemma she felt. They couldn't let Sasha get away with bullying them into complicity—but was it really okay to threaten her back? Even if the circumstances were this extreme? It didn't *feel* right, that was for sure.

Maddie finally began to wonder: Was there another way?

CHAPTER 17

JACK

Jack's last class of the day was Spanish, where he filled out a worksheet on verbs, then handed it in so he could spend the final fifteen minutes of class drawing. He had an idea for a new sketch and his fingers itched to start working on it. If it went well, Jack would ask if he could put it up in the Gala art show, replacing one of his other works.

It was a drawing of Mom in her college softball uniform, stepping up to the plate. It was based on one of the many Mom photos in their home, which Jack had looked at so many times they were imprinted on his brain, this one part of a set from the first year Mom's team won the College World Series of softball. Drawing Mom was nothing new. But wanting to share the drawing with his family? That was a newly hatched chick, still unsteady on its legs. But it was growing.

Jack had not stopped thinking about what Maddie and Nora had said: that if Jack was excited about his art, Dad and Matt would be too. Could it be true? Jack's thinking had gotten snarled up in his brain, putting the fear of being regarded as wimpy on his family when in fact that was a fear that came from inside Jack. He hadn't seen that in a small, closed-off part of himself, Jack worried it was a bit wimpy to wield a pencil instead of a bat. Now that he was examining it, it was losing its power. And Jack had realized something else: Sharing his art with his family and hearing their enthusiasm would make Jack proud. That was something he wanted. So here he was, working on a new picture to display in the Gala and actually getting excited to share his Gala display with Dad and Matt.

How things had changed since this morning, when he had snuck into the building, ready to rip down his pictures.

Jack bent over the paper, the pencil an extension of his hand as he etched out the contours of the bat, the way Mom's fingers gripped it, sure and strong. Everything else fell away as Jack's hand moved across the page. He was so lost in his work that the final bell made him jerk up in his seat, the pencil falling onto the floor.

Michelle B., who sat next to him, laughed, though

not unkindly, as she bent down to grab the pencil, which was rolling under her desk.

"You were in the zone," she said. Jack knew this was something sports people said and he appreciated her using it for his art. She glanced down at his paper. "Whoa, Jack, that is incredible."

Jack smiled shyly. "It's my mom."

"She looks like the real deal," Michelle B. said, heading out.

"She was," Jack said to himself. He slid the paper carefully into his backpack, which he had brought to class so he'd get to Emma's locker fast, without making a stop at his. And remembering this had him hurrying out of the room.

"Jack, are you coming in?" Avi asked as Jack passed the art room. Jack almost always went to the art room after school—art club met twice a week, and Ms. Antonov often stayed late the rest of the week so students could come in and work on their own.

"I have something to do, but hopefully after that," Jack said. It would be helpful to get feedback from his art friends and teacher on his drawing of Mom—but obviously dealing with Sasha came first.

Nora, Henry, and Maddie were just outside the

crowded B alcove when Jack arrived. "Hey," he said, and smiled. He was surprised how happy he was to see them.

Henry was bouncing about Tigger-like, Nora was rummaging through her satchel (so odd), and Maddie cleared her throat when she saw him.

"So listen," Maddie began, at the same time Henry said, "It's time to take down the Wicked Witch of Snow Valley!"

Maddie glared at him. Henry held up his hands. "What, that's what we're doing, isn't it?"

"I thought so too," Jack said, puzzled by Maddie's reaction. "What's up?"

"We shouldn't take anyone down," she said, poking Henry in the shoulder when he howled at this. "Hear me out. I am not saying we hand over the folder or give in to what she wants—obviously. But I don't want to do what Geneva did and what Sasha's doing now—threats, blackmail. I want us to be better than that."

Henry moaned. "Come on, she has it coming."

Jack wasn't sure—no one deserved to be blackmailed. But would anything else work? If they did nothing, Sasha would get away with threatening all of them to get what she wanted.

"Watch it!" Nora bellowed as three boys barreled past, one of them hitting her with his elbow.

"Sorry," the guy called back sheepishly.

"And you really think because you're short no one will take you seriously," Jack couldn't help saying.

Maddie and Henry both laughed at this, and Nora couldn't hide a smile.

"The thing is though," Maddie said, her face intense as she went back to Sasha, "she doesn't have it coming. No one should feel like we've been made to feel today. We can find a way to not let her get away with it, but not be total bullies either."

"Find some nuance," Nora said appreciatively.

"I hate nuance," Henry grumbled.

"Do you even know what it means?" Maddie asked, hands on her hips.

"What does that have to do with it?" Henry sulked.

Was it strange that five hours ago this would have irked Jack to no end but now he found Henry's silly remarks kind of funny? Yeah, it was strange—but then, everything about this day had been pretty strange.

"So what do you think we should do?" Jack asked Maddie. The alcove was clearing out as people headed to clubs, sports, or home. Sasha would arrive any second. Jack also knew Henry needed to get back before the bus brought his siblings home, though that wasn't for another forty-five minutes.

"We appeal to her better nature," Maddie said.

Henry scoffed. "Sasha doesn't have one of those."

Jack was worried Henry was right. Or that if it was there, it was buried too deep.

Maddie glared at Henry as Nora spoke up. "We can try if you really think it could work," she said.

Maddie nodded.

"But if it doesn't work, we offer her a trade," Jack said quickly. Because he too was willing to give Maddie's idea a try, but he wasn't willing to walk out of the meeting with any risk that Matt's secret would *ever* be revealed.

"What kind of trade?" Maddie asked.

Jack waited while a couple of girls from drama club hurried by.

"We keep her secret, she keeps ours and goes to the office to free Louis," Jack said.

"Isn't that kind of like blackmail?" Maddie asked, her brows scrunching up.

Jack was starting to feel annoyed. "Why are you so worried about Sasha's feelings after everything she did?" he snapped.

"Seriously," Henry agreed, pulling at his hair.

"I just don't want to be mean," Maddie said quietly.

Nora raised a hand before either of the boys could respond. "None of us do, but if we don't handle this, a lot of people are going to get hurt. Including the four of us."

"Yeah, it's meaner to let Louis get expelled, expose Emma's secret, and give Sasha the power to tell everyone about Jack's brother and my dad next time she wants something from us," Henry said.

Maddie nodded. Sometimes Henry really made a lot of sense and obviously this was true. But Jack could see how much it bothered her to be unkind, and his annoyance slipped away.

"A trade is kind of like threatening her, I get it," he said gently. "But remember, we're not using what we know to make her do something unfair or awful. Which is what Geneva did to Sasha and Sasha's been doing to us. Maybe it is kind of blackmail, but we're not forcing her to do something—we're pressuring her to *undo* something, something she did."

Nora nodded. "Jack's right: We're not making her do anything that will hurt her. We're just asking her to stop blackmailing people."

"It will hurt her to have to give up performing in the Gala and to get in trouble for all she did," Maddie said. She was shifting her weight from one foot to the other and twirling her ponytail around her fingers. Clearly she was worked up about this.

"But that's *her* fault—she set those things in motion, not us," Jack pointed out. He could tell Maddie agreed when she let her hair fall back over her shoulder. "All we're doing is making sure she's stopped from hurting more people. And if that means she gets consequences for things she did, that's on her, not us. We didn't make her gather Emma's work or secrets about other students—she decided to do it and use it to blackmail people. And there should be consequences for that!"

"Also," Nora said, her lips slightly pursed, like she was thinking as she spoke, "Geneva told us two things about Sasha: her mom's history and the fact that Sasha got suspended. Sasha would hate for either of those things to get out, so I say we just choose one: the part about Sasha, but not the part about her mom. Because that is seriously *no one's* business."

"We'd never actually tell," Jack said. "We won't have to."

"But she should know we won't hold her mom's past over her head, not ever," Nora said fiercely. "Because that is wrong—it's seriously wrong."

Jack had never paused to consider this—but Nora was right.

"Astrid has a point," Henry said with a grin.

Nora rolled her eyes, but she grinned too.

Jack looked at Maddie. "So we're agreed that we'll promise not to tell about her mom, no matter what. But the suspension is something she made happen, it's something she did, so it's fair game. I mean, I don't think we'd ever have to use it—but we need something to bargain with to stop Sasha's rampage of terror."

Henry snickered at this, but Maddie just nodded slowly. "Okay, but can we at least try appealing to her better nature first?"

"Sure," Henry said, clearly certain it wouldn't work.

"And if it doesn't, we offer the trade," Maddie agreed. She didn't look happy but she didn't look as anxious as before either.

"We could also consider throwing in a few extra

asks," Henry said, grinning. "Like cleaning out our lockers and—"

"Ha-ha," Maddie said, rolling her eyes. But Jack, who was grinning, saw her smile as she turned away.

"Are we ready?" Henry asked.

Jack nodded vigorously, Nora nodded calmly, and Maddie hesitated, then nodded too. She opened her bag and took out Sasha's silver backpack.

Nora pulled the now-empty folder out of her satchel and gave it to Maddie, who put it in Sasha's pack. And then they headed to locker alcove A.

Sasha smiled when she saw them—or maybe she was just smiling at the sight of her backpack. "I'm glad you've come to your senses," she said. "I'll take that now." She held out a hand.

Maddie passed it over and Sasha, displaying zero faith in them, immediately unzipped it, pulled out the folder, then scowled. "Are you kidding me?" she barked. "Give me the papers that were in here. All of them."

Jack felt himself stiffen at her tone.

"That's not going to happen," Maddie said calmly. "And, Sasha, I don't think that's what you want either. I think you know this is mean."

Sasha looked at Maddie as if Maddie had lost her mind. "I play to win," she said, like it was obvious.

Which, actually, it was.

"But do you want to win like this, tearing people down and hurting them?" Maddie asked, stepping forward, her hands out. "I don't think this is really who you are."

Sasha gave Maddie a hard look. "You don't know anything about me. Who I am is a winner. The best. And I'll do what it takes to stay on top." She flipped back her shiny hair to emphasize her words, nearly hitting Maddie in the face.

"But—" Maddie began.

"Stop wasting my time and give me those papers," Sasha said sharply, her eyes ice.

Maddie's shoulders slumped and she stepped back. Jack reached out to pat her arm. While Sasha may not have had a better nature, Maddie did—and hers was awesome.

"You're not getting the papers," Henry told Sasha. His voice was even but Jack saw how his eyes sparkled. It *did* feel good to know that Sasha would never have the power to hurt anyone in that folder—or the four of them—again.

"Then the four of you are going down, along with Louis and his loser sister," Sasha announced.

"That's not happening either," Nora said, just as evenly.

"Actually that's exactly what's happening," Sasha snapped. Her cheeks were no longer a golden pink—they were now a blotchy red.

"Let me tell you why it's not," Henry said. "And why it's in your interest to hear us out."

Sasha went still, so still it was creepy. Her face was rapidly going from red to an unnatural gray, and Jack could hear the sound of her breath quickening. "You know about what happened in Oak Ridge," she said, her voice eerily dead.

"Yes, and we would never tell about your mom—not ever," Nora said quickly.

"Right," Sasha said bitterly, "like I believe that."

"We mean it," Maddie said, so passionately Jack thought Sasha *had* to believe it.

"But you know all about my suspension too," Sasha said in the same awful tone. "And people here finding out what I did—it would ruin me."

"We're not threatening you," Maddie said quickly, reaching out a hand to touch Sasha.

Sasha jerked back forcefully. "That's sure what it looks like," she said. "And do not touch me." Her breathing was unsteady and her hands were shaking.

Jack finally saw why Maddie had wanted to do this as gently as possible: Sasha was clearly traumatized.

"We really aren't," Jack said, his voice soft. "We just want to make a deal—a swap. We keep your secret, you keep ours, you get Louis out of trouble and—"

"And none of us ever speak of this again," Henry finished. Jack could tell just by the way Henry said it that he saw what Jack saw—and that he didn't want to hurt Sasha either.

"Why should I trust you?" Sasha asked.

"Because we all have something to gain from this and we all lose if one side bails," Henry said. "So if we each keep our mouths shut, everyone wins."

"I guess," Sasha said grudgingly. "Okay, I won't say anything about what I know, but that's it. Louis and Emma aren't part of the deal."

"Yes, they are," Nora said forcefully. "And you're giving Emma that spot on the Gala squad—it's hers and she earned it."

"No," Sasha said with such fury Jack took a step back. "That spot is mine—there's no way I'm letting it go."

"It's not though," Maddie said quietly. "You didn't earn it—you threatened one of your teammates to make her sacrifice it."

"I am performing in the Gala, end of story." Sasha crossed her arms over her chest.

"It won't help," Nora said.

"What?" Sasha asked.

"It won't undo what Geneva did to you or how you got chased off your old team," Maddie said. "Nothing can undo that."

Sasha was suddenly blinking a lot. Henry glanced at Jack in alarm, and Jack returned his stricken gaze. Was Sasha actually going to cry?

"I want them to see me on Tansy Mink's channel," Sasha whispered, her voice quivery.

So many shocking things had taken place in the past few hours but this most definitely took the cake. Not just that Sasha was breaking down in tears, but that Jack actually felt bad for her.

"The spot is Emma's," Maddie said quietly.

"I hate you all," Sasha spat out, and then she whirled around.

"Wait, where are you going?" Henry asked, sounding slightly panicked.

"Where do you think I'm going, idiot?" Sasha hissed, venom oozing from her voice. "To the office to get your stupid friend Louis off and ruin my chances at ever being in a Gala because you guys are making me do it!"

"We're not—" Jack began, but Sasha was storming off.

"I hate you!" she shouted one last time.

Then she stomped around the corner and was gone.

CHAPTER 18

HENRY

"So I guess our work here is done," Henry said as they walked out the front entrance of Snow Valley Secondary School. They'd stopped by the office to make sure Sasha followed through, as well as to let Louis know they had Emma's things. The air was icy crisp but the sun was warm on Henry's cheeks. It seemed as though years had passed since he'd walked up these steps this morning. And boy, had a lot changed.

"We should wait for Louis, to give him back Emma's work," Nora said. "And make sure he's okay." She scuffed through some fallen leaves as they headed down the path to a bench under an oak tree.

"Also . . ." Maddie said as she, Jack, and Nora sat. Henry had some extra energy, so he stayed upright, bouncing a little. "I have some unfinished business with you."

She was looking at Henry and he stopped bouncing.

"That stuff you told us about your dad losing the job because of you," she began.

"I'm fine, let's not talk about it," Henry said quickly. The lightness in his shoulders that had arrived when Sasha stalked off to the office was replaced by lead.

"Henry, that was not your fault," Maddie said firmly. She had her hands held out in front of her to emphasize the point.

"Not even a little," Jack chimed in.

"Yes, it was," Henry said. Why did they not see the obvious? "My dad missed the interview because I was late coming home to watch Lacey and George. What was he going to do, bring them along?"

"Sure," Nora said, shrugging. "People get that child care falls through at the last minute. Even on a job interview."

"He could have asked someone else to watch them too, a neighbor or something," Jack added. "My dad had to do that a few times when I was too little to stay on my own and he had something big at the college."

Henry suddenly needed to sit. Because this—what they had just said—was actually what was obvious. But he'd never seen it before. "Dad said he couldn't go because he had to watch the kids."

"That was the excuse he used, but I bet he'd have come up with another if you'd been home on time,"

Maddie said. At first Henry did not understand why she spoke so gently and why both Jack and Nora were looking at him with concern, but then the pieces came together.

"You're saying Dad didn't want the job," he said. "But he did—he said so."

The three of them were quiet. "He did, he said it," Henry repeated. But his mind was traveling back to the week before the interview. Mom had said Dad wanted the job. Henry, George, and Lacey too. But had Dad said it? And if he had, had he meant it? Henry always recalled that as a good week, when everyone was feeling hopeful about the future. But was he remembering wrong? Was it possible that just he, Mom, Lacey, and George felt hopeful and Dad just felt like staying in bed?

"But why wouldn't Dad want that job?" Henry asked in a small voice.

"Henry, I think your dad is depressed," Maddie said.

"No, he's not," Henry said. "Dad was never sad like this before Covid and everything."

"So maybe it's situational," Maddie said. And now all three of them were looking at her.

"What was that, Doctor?" Jack asked.

Maddie grinned and brushed back a lock of hair that was blowing over her face. "My stepmom is a psychiatrist and we talk a lot about mental illness because she says people don't talk about it enough."

"Why?" Nora asked.

"It makes people uncomfortable," Maddie explained.

"Like talking about racism," Jack said. He'd pulled a pencil out of his bag and was running it between his palms.

"Yeah, good point," Maddie agreed. "With mental illness no one wants to admit they aren't perfect, even though none of us are. And if you can't admit you need help, like Jack's brother did, then you don't get better."

"So you can get better?" Henry asked. Because unlike Maddie, he was no expert, but Dad staying in bed for a year seemed like something that might not be fixable. But what if it was? What if Dad getting help could, well, help? And get him to start being Dad again.

"Yeah, totally," Maddie said, like it was no big thing. "It's treatable if you treat it."

Henry was quiet, taking this in.

"Getting help changed Matt's life," Jack said. "Mine and Dad's too."

That sounded good. Really, really good.

"Give me your number," Maddie said, pulling out her phone. "I'll text you Charlotte's work information—she'll be happy to talk to you and your family about it. She's cool like that."

Jack pulled out his phone. "Maybe we should all exchange numbers," he said.

"Why?" Henry asked.

Jack looked at Henry like Henry was a fool. "So we can hang out sometimes."

"Oh," Henry said, a huge smile suddenly taking over his face. "Yeah, you're right, we should."

Just like that, Henry had new friends.

It really had been a day. And it was about to be even more of a day because pushing his way out of the big metal doors of the school, his brown hair blowing in the breeze as he blinked and glanced toward the sky, as if he never thought he'd see the sun again, was Louis.

CHAPTER 19

NORA

Louis had spotted them and he hurried down the steps, then jogged over.

"You guys saved me," he said. He'd said the same thing when they had turned up in the office.

"Yeah, we did," Henry agreed. He was up and bouncing around again. "You can think of us as superheroes."

Louis smiled as Nora rolled her eyes. "Or not," she said, reaching into her satchel for the stack of Emma's work. "These belong to your sister. We didn't read them; we just kept them safe."

"Thanks," Louis said, taking the papers from Nora and shaking his head. "Seriously, I don't know how you guys did it, but this is incredible. Emma is going to be so happy to get her stuff back—she was losing her mind over it—she wouldn't come to school and was barely talking. We were all pretty worried about her."

"I'm glad we could help," Nora said. It was an understatement—she was thrilled they'd managed to stop a blackmailer in her tracks—and done it nicely. Well, as nicely as they could.

"You really did," Louis said, rubbing his face for a moment. "I could've been expelled and now all I have is four days of in-school suspension for breaking into Sasha's locker and taking her bag. Well, and dealing with my parents, who are pretty angry at me and Emma for not coming to them. But that's a lot better than expulsion!"

It definitely was. Nora imagined that breaking into a locker usually had bigger consequences—but given the extreme extenuating circumstances, this punishment made sense.

"Do you know if Emma got her spot back in the Gala?" Maddie asked. She had set her hair free and it blew gently in the breeze.

Louis nodded. "Yeah, after Sasha confessed, Principal Montenegro said Sasha had lost her spot on the Gala squad. She was calling Coach Faizal about it when I left. You guys fixed everything."

Nora could not help smiling in satisfaction at this response. But there was one more thing that had to be said. "Emma shouldn't feel ashamed about having a learning disability. Tons of people have them."

"My dad does," Jack added, pulling out his drawing pad.

"Really? Coach Tran?" Louis was obviously surprised. He shifted his pack so he could open it but was looking at Jack.

"Yup," Jack said, eyes on the page he'd flipped to that had small drawings of oak leaves, each exquisite. "Emma can ask him about it if she wants. His doctor once said part of why he coaches so well is that he sees things other people don't—because his brain works a little differently—not better or worse, just differently."

Louis shook his head. "Thanks, but I don't know—she'd be intimidated. Our family is pretty serious about the Cougars."

Jack's pride at this was evident in the way he grinned. "That's an even better reason for her to talk to him. He's always home on Sundays—you guys can come by anytime. But be prepared—he thinks he makes the world's best pancakes, but those things are like bricks and he will make you try them."

Louis smiled. "I think we could handle that. Thanks."

This was nice but Nora decided to push for more. "You could also talk to him at the Gala. He'll be the one admiring the art." She gave Jack a pointed look. A very pointed look.

And she was pleased when Jack nodded. "Yeah, he will," he said, smiling. "I have a lot of stuff to show him and my brother."

"Cool," Louis said. He was stuffing Emma's papers in his backpack and didn't notice the looks exchanged between Nora, Maddie, and Henry at this news. The looks of total delight.

"One other thing," Jack said. "You should write to Astrid to ask for more information about learning disabilities and why they're no big thing. Astrid knows a lot."

"About everything," Henry added, grinning slyly at Nora.

So Nora gave in. "It's a pretty good column."

"Pretty great," Maddie corrected immediately.

"Yeah, it might be pretty great," Nora said. The warm feeling was nestled in her chest.

"I think whoever writes it should be pretty proud of themselves," Maddie said.

Nora grinned. "You're right," she said. "It's work to be proud of."

Maddie beamed, though Louis looked confused.

The breeze picked up, loosening a few leaves from the oak branches that fluttered down around them.

"I love Astrid," Louis said. "But even she couldn't have helped me today, not like you guys did."

Nora saw the others work not to laugh out loud at this.

"I'm going to go to art club," Jack said. "I have a drawing I want some feedback on."

Maddie stood up. "I should get to dance practice—I'm already in hot water with Coach." But Nora could see she wasn't worried, now that the threat of Sasha's video had been erased.

"I have a column I need to start," Nora said, pulling her satchel over her shoulder and standing up as well.

"You know," Henry said, hoisting on his pack as they all headed back to the path, "this started out as one of the worst days ever but it's ended up being pretty great."

Jack nodded. "Yeah, and who would have predicted it?"

Maddie smiled. "Astrid maybe," she said. "And yeah, a very good day."

Nora looked at her new friends and she too smiled. "The best," she said. "It's been the best."

ACKNOWLEDGMENTS

My agent, Sara Crowe, is the best cheerleader and champion an author could hope for, and I am supremely lucky to be working with her and fabulous Team Pip: Cameron, Rakeem, Ashley, Holly, and Elena. I am just as lucky in my Scholastic team: Emily Seife is the editor authors dream of, discovering every scrap of potential in my stories and helping me realize them all. Designer Maeve Norton gifted me with a cover I adore, and production editor Janell Harris made sure we stayed the path to a gorgeous final product. I am so grateful to publicist Alex Kelleher-Nagorski for finding every opportunity to share my books and for being such a joy to work with. I tell my students that I too make typos and spelling errors on a regular basis, something copy editor Priscilla Eakeley and proofreaders Lara Kennedy, Nicole Ortiz, and Jackie Hornberger can attest to—I am indebted to them for their care, time, and attention to ensure we corrected every single one.

When I am not writing, I have the great fortune to serve as the part-time librarian at PS 32. Shout-outs to the amazing students, staff, and families who welcomed me, and extra loud shout-outs to my ally from day one, Stephen Grecco; my fabulous library buddy, Perniece Roper; the ladies who know it all, Ms. Johnson and Ms. Lisa; and Denise Watson-Adin, who inspires me daily with her leadership and heart.

In the business of writing and the business of life, I rely on the incredible friendships of Marianna Baer, Kira Bazile, Debbi Michiko Florence, Donna Freitas, Lisa Graff, Deborah Heiligman, Carolyn MacCullough, Alexa Murphy, Josh Phillips, Marie Rutkoski, Jill Santopolo, Eliot Schrefer, Rebecca Stead, and Martin Wilson. I would be lost without them!

And I would have been lost long ago without my sister, lifelong partner, and the funniest person I know (after our dad), Sam. My brother, Nghia, and most glorious nephews, Khai, Avi, Shiloh, and Dash, bring me endless joy, and hugs to Kim, whose devoted readership is more than I deserve. My heart belongs to Greg, Ainyr, and Erlan, to whom I happily promise a lifetime of yummy brunches, exciting travels, and nosy questions if I suspect that you may in fact be lying!

ABOUT THE AUTHOR

Daphne Benedis-Grab is the author of the middle-grade novels *The Angel Tree*, *Clementine for Christmas*, *Army Brats*, and *I Know Your Secret*, as well as the young adult book *The Girl in the Wall*. She is the part-time school librarian at PS 32 in Brooklyn, where she gets to hang out with kids and books all day (she is a very lucky person!). She lives in New York City with her husband, two teens, and a cat who has been known to sit on her computer if he feels she has been typing too long. Visit her at daphnebg.com.

TURN THE PAGE FOR A SNEAK PEEK OF
I KNOW YOUR SECRET!

CHAPTER 1

SUNDAY: 5:30 P.M.
OWEN

It was random that Owen even checked his email before dinner that Sunday. Usually he went straight from pickup basketball with the guys to the backyard. His stepdad, Big Rob, was still insisting it was warm enough for Sunday night barbecues. Which was fine with Owen—give him a pile of ribs soaked in Big Rob's secret Lexington sauce and he would be happy eating outside in January. But Mom said barbecue season in upstate New York ended with the first frost—which had been that morning.

So when Owen got home, Big Rob was standing next to the cold grill, saying, "It was more a light dusting of rain, not an actual frost," while Mom countered that rain did not leave a white icy residue.

Owen figured it would be a while before the family ate anything, so he went into Mom's office to use the computer. His older sister, Jade (who was technically his stepsister), normally hogged it, but Jade was on a college tour with her mom and away for the week. So the computer was free for Owen and the project he had started during the Covid-19 shutdown.

It wasn't something he had told anyone—right now it was just his. But Owen was creating a graphic novel. None of his friends were into comics, drawing, or writing, and while Big Rob was enthused about most of Owen's interests, Mom and Dad were more invested in Owen's grades, which were somewhat less than great. They didn't nag him much, but Owen knew they might butt in if they realized that half the time they thought Owen was doing homework, he was actually working on his story.

Owen had reached a point in the book where he needed to know a little more about the armor worn by samurai for when his character went back in time. He did a quick search, found some great images, and then, while they were printing, logged into his account.

And that was how he ended up being the first of the four to see the email.

6:15 P.M.
GEMMA

"Can I please be excused?" Gemma asked, doing her best to appear casual. This was hard because she was pretty much crawling out of her skin. But it was essential that Mom not see how desperate Gemma was to get on her phone after Mom's new "screen-free Sundays." Mom was still scarred by all the screen time Gemma, Kate, and Avi had had during the Covid-19 shutdown. Although it'd been necessary for school and to socialize online, now that things were open again and people could go out, Gemma's mom was determined to keep them off screens as much as possible.

"Isn't it your night to load the dishwasher?" Gemma's evil younger sister, Kate, asked.

"No, it's Avi's," Gemma said between gritted teeth. Her older brother, who was as sweet as Kate was evil, nodded cheerfully.

"Okay, then," Mom said, sounding reluctant.

"I did all my homework," Gemma said, smiling like she wasn't aching to snatch her phone out of the charging cabinet and fly up to her room.

"Great, off you go," Dad said, waving Gemma toward the living room.

It took everything in her but she managed to walk calmly to the cabinet, take out the phone without checking it (Mom was watching), and meander to the stairs. She didn't start running until she was half-way up and Kate had started moaning about how she hated her math teacher.

And after all that? *He* hadn't even texted.

Gemma threw herself down on her pink comforter-covered bed (so immature, but Mom wouldn't get her a new one until high school, which was years away) and scrolled through her notifications, then went to her inbox. She noticed the email right away and not because the subject line was all caps. Gemma noticed it right away because of what it said.

I KNOW YOUR SECRET

Todd wanted to punch the computer screen.

He could imagine how it would feel to put his fist through the screen, blasting that email apart—but obviously he didn't. Mom was so proud of the old desktop her boss had given her that it sat in a place of honor on the kitchen table where they ate. Todd knew Mom's boss just wanted to get rid of the computer without hassle since it was ancient, but the important thing was that Mom didn't know that. And it did still work. Even though it took up half the small table in their very small trailer.

"I forgot my milk," Mom said, coming out of her bedroom. She was getting ready to watch her Sunday shows.

Todd quickly closed the email before she could see what was on the screen.

"You know how it helps me relax." She was wearing what she called her "cozy robe," her feet in the bunny slippers Todd had gotten her for her birthday. Mom loved bunnies and wore the slippers every night.

"Want me to get it for you?" Todd asked. He started

to stand up and found he felt shaky, almost dizzy, from what he'd just read.

"No, you keep doing your work on the computer," Mom said, grabbing a teacup and saucer for her milk. It was the "little touches," as she called them, that made Mom happy. That and anything involving bunnies, Todd, or chocolate.

As soon as Mom was safely back in her room, Todd clicked back to the email. As he read it a second time, his fists clenched up.

But punching wasn't going to help him get out of this:

> *I know your secret. Do what I say, when I say it, and I won't tell a soul. Skip even one step and I will tell everyone. Text me at this number as soon as you read this email. And then get ready for tomorrow. It's going to be a very big day.*

Ally's hands were shaking, her breath coming in short, sharp bursts as she shoved things around on her desk, trying to find her phone so she could send the text. Thank goodness she had checked her email tonight! It had been a long day helping Grandpa and Gram—Sundays were always long days, not that Ally minded. Nothing mattered more to her than the animals at the sanctuary she helped her grandparents run. And nothing made her, or her grandparents, happier.

But still, the work was tiring. Often after evening animal feeding and cuddles, Ally took a long, hot shower, fell into bed with a book, and passed out by nine. And what if she had done that tonight and missed this email?

It was too awful to even contemplate.

She finally found her phone, wedged into a far corner of the desk under a pile of *Cat Care* magazines. It took two tries to open up a new message and type in the phone number from the email. Then she hesitated. What was the proper response when someone was blackmailing you? She settled on *It's Ally* and pressed send. Then she waited, cold sweat slithering down her sides, staring at her phone.

Ally had no idea who could be threatening her like this. And how had they found out her secret? It was most certainly the one thing Ally never, ever wanted anyone to know. Because if anyone found out what she had done—

Her stomach tumbled ominously as a bubble appeared on the screen, three dots flashing. Ally closed her eyes and said a quick prayer. This person—whoever they were—had the power to ruin everything Ally had ever truly loved.